My
Perfect Life
At
Cornish Cottage

By
S J Crabb

For Debbie & Sue
May you both find your own
perfect lives x

Chapter One

I am woken up by the usual sound of my husband's bodily functions emanating from the en suite.

I find it strangely comforting and fleetingly wonder if it would work as a design concept for an alarm clock. I mean surely I'm not alone; there must be millions of women waking up to the familiar sounds every day.

I suppose it's the human equivalent of a cock crowing.

Keeping my eyes tightly shut I hear him coming back into the room. If I can just make it five more minutes then he will be off downstairs and I will be spared from the morning grope.

How is it best to feign sleep? I mean I should probably throw in a little snort or a snore, maybe thrash around a bit and perfect some rapid eye movement. Instead I lie here like a frozen statue, tense and in tune to every last bodily function that he makes.

I can sense him approaching my side of the bed, the one that I have occupied for the last twenty years of our marriage. Strange how territorial we all get over a certain side. Even when we go on holiday we adopt the same procedures, it becomes "*My Side*."

Now he is hovering beside me and I run my tongue around my teeth trying to dispel my morning breath. What if he wants a session before work? I wonder if I could fit it in before the school run.

I feel a gentle tap on my arm and he whispers, "Sophie, are you awake?"

I wonder how to open my eyes.

Should I adopt the wanton sex kitten pose or the irate bored housewife/ downtrodden wife and mother pose?

He taps my arm again and says louder, "Sophie, wake up I need to say something."

Well this is different, it looks like I will be spared from a marathon session - I say marathon more like a gentle jog on his part before falling at the first hurdle. Stamina has never been his strong point.

My eyes snap open and I take in the sight of my husband of the last twenty years. Slightly wider with a lot less hair than when I first met him, sporting the grey hair that becomes distinguished on a man and screams pensioner on a woman.

He looks at me with a worried expression and I sit up now extremely curious.

"What's the matter darling, can't you find a matching pair of socks? I'm sure there are some in the utility room."

He looks down and sits on the bed next to me, perching on the edge as if he is afraid that I will bite. I shift into an upright position and once again wonder what it could be.

If I'm taking bets it's probably something to do with my birthday. I am going to be forty in a few weeks time and he has been hinting at a surprise for the last few months.

Suddenly I feel excited. Maybe he has booked us a mini break without Harry and Mr Tumnus. Gosh I can't remember the last time we did something on our own. When you have a six year old and a cocker spaniel they do take up quite a bit of your time. Feeling happy at the thought I smile at him and prepare myself to act surprised when he springs the treat on me.

He starts fiddling with his hands which he always does when he is nervous and I detect a flush creeping over his neck. He looks at me and I see that he is genuinely nervous and a sudden fear grips me.

Oh no he must have a terrible illness. Maybe that visit to the doctors last week was bad news. He might have an incurable illness and only have months to live. I could be widowed and have to bring up Harry on my own. Oh my god I don't suit black and even worse I might have to actually join the rat race and work 9-5. My anxiety levels are now on code red and reaching out I grasp his hand gently.

"What's the matter Lysander, you're worrying me."

He shifts away almost as if he can't bear me to touch him and then appears to steel himself to deliver the bad news. Turning towards me he fixes me with a blank stare and says in a loud determined voice, "I'm sorry Sophie but I've met someone else and I want a divorce."

For a moment I think that I must be still asleep. I sit still and just stare at him whilst my mind struggles to compute this unusual information. I blink rapidly in the hope that every time I re-focus he will have two heads and the body of a wildebeest.

I mean surely I am dreaming because we don't even argue.

He looks at me anxiously. "Do you understand Sophie? I'm sorry but I can't pretend anymore. It's not fair on any of us and I can't go on living a lie."

My hand flies up to my mouth as if I can't be trusted to form a coherent sentence. My mind is spinning and I suppose I must be in shock because surely I should be crying and screaming and bashing him over the head with the industrial torch that I keep under the bed for emergencies in case of power cuts or intruders.

They don't sell Tasers in Robert Dyas and now I can see why as I know that I would be very much using it on him right now and I wouldn't even issue the obligatory "*Taser- Taser*" warning before I let him have it.

He shakes his head and stands up awkwardly.

"Listen I can see that you need time to get your head around what I have just told you and I am running late for the office. We will talk later and iron everything out then. I just want to say that it's not you it's me and I have changed. I am sure that when you come to terms with it you will see that it's for the best.

Well at least it's out in the open now. Anyway sorry to have to run but you know life goes on as they say. I'll let Mr Tumnus out when I go downstairs; just remember not to leave him out there too long as I still haven't mended that hole in the fence at the end."

And then he is gone.

Chapter Two

I am still sitting in the same place when a little body comes flying into the room and jumps on to the bed. "Mummy, Mummy I didn't mean it and Fireman Sam has wetted the bed again with his hose."

I look down at the gorgeous bundle of love that is my son Harry. Large gentle brown eyes look up at me carrying the weight of the world in them as he looks at me anxiously. I just about understand what he just said and pull him to me tightly and stroke his soft brown hair that never seems to sit straight.

"Don't worry baby boy, we'll send in the cleaning troll. Do you need to use the toilet now?"

He grips me tightly and says quietly, "No thank you, I think that it's all gone now."

My heart tightens as I sit holding my little boy. Six years old and about to discover that his little world has fallen apart. I blink back the tears and set my resolve in place. Not now, he can have at least one more day of happiness. I will make sure that he is fine, my momma bear is rushing to the fore and now my little boy is the most important thing in my life.

I paste a smile on to my face and tickle him stupid. The sound of his laughter is like a knife to my heart and I feel a sudden rush of hatred for my soon to be ex-husband.

How could he do this to his son? The thought of what is now in my future is almost too much to bear, so I push it all away and start the process of totally overcompensating my son.

"How about I make you loads of sticky sugary American pancakes for breakfast like they do on the television?" His screams of joy give me the answer I need and he grabs my hand in excitement and bounds from the bed. "Can I eat them in my spaceman suit?" I nod. "Of course you can Mr Astronaut. Whilst you get suited up I will head off to mission control and prepare for lift off." He hurries from the room and leaves me to get a grip.

I'm actually not sure how I get through the morning ritual of pre-school activity which usually involves lots of shouting on my part towards an unruly dog and an errant child.

However this morning they could draw on the walls, rip up the carpet and slide down the stairs on a mattress for all I care because there is only one thing buzzing around in my mind, "Why me?" I mean couples separate all the time; in our village the single parents outnumber the married ones. I have always felt somewhat smug as I looked around at my own cosy stereotypical middle class family and felt sorry for the more dysfunctional ones around me. It's all coming back to bite me now with a vengeance though and the tears burn behind my eyes at how quickly my cosy bubble has burst.

Harry doesn't appear to sense anything different and is more interested in gathering his Transformers together to take to school.

Soon we are somehow ready and I start the short walk to the village school.

Harry holds my hand and chatters incessantly on the way whilst Mr Tumnus tries to stop at every wall and corner to sniff the evidence of his friends that have already made the journey. Normally Harry and I would be singing a little song as we go - usually the theme tune to Postman Pat which I am strangely addicted to.

Today though I can't focus on anything else but the sound of my world coming crashing down around me.

We join the line of other parents heading towards the school gates and I feel as if I am having an out of body experience because everything looks the same as usual but it is now very different. It is as though I am seeing everything through someone else's eyes and nothing appears real anymore.

Harry sees his friend Edward and drops my hand and races towards him. As I draw near I take in the welcoming smile of his mother, my best friend Simone.

Seeing her friendly face causes mine to fall and at once I can see the concern in her eyes. She leans forward and whispers, "What's the matter Sophie has someone died or something you look...well shell shocked if I'm honest." I just stare at her in disbelief and then somehow manage to squeak, "Lysander wants a divorce." I see the shock register in her face and she grabs hold of my arm. "Right this is what you must do. Act normal and pretend you're someone else for the next ten minutes, I don't know Anthea Turner or someone perfect like that, do what you have to do and then once the prison gates close you and I are going to yours to work out the next step. Ok?"

I nod numbly and summon my inner Anthea to the fore and paste a happy sugary smile on to my face as I approach the battle ground otherwise known as the playground.

Simone walks next to me as if she is my minder and with a similar expression on her face we contemplate the dreaded Playground Mums.

All around us is perfect housewife perfection. Yummy mummy land with more cutting out stakes than an origami factory. These women take no prisoners. They smell out your fear and your insecurities and they gorge on scandal and gossip. If these women knew of my new situation they would pounce on me and feed off of it stripping me to the bone until there is nothing left of me. Simone is right; I need to keep up the appearance of Stepford perfection for as long as possible.

The noise of the children playing is almost deafening and the chatter of the mums adds to the chaos. I look around me at the sea of Cath Kidston and Boden clad warriors who use their designer prams as battering rams to gain the coveted spot by the office doors- because that is where *he* lives.

Almost on cue the door opens and there is an audible gasp of excitement as all eyes swivel towards the god that is Mr Rainford the year 2 teacher.

Simone tenses up beside me and if we were in a film this is the part that would appear in slow motion cueing the latest love song as he emerges from his lair.

Mr Rainford is not your typical teacher. He looks as if he has stepped out of an advert for men's underpants. He has a chiselled jaw that shows a hint of stubble. His eyes are brown and sexy and when he looks at you you feel as if you are the only person in the room. His clothes are immaculate and he moves with swagger to his step.

There is not a mother here including myself that probably hasn't fantasised about him at some point. The trouble is I think he's gay.

He looks around him with amusement and then rings the bell that he holds aloft as if it is an Olympic torch. There is a stampede of children as they fall into their lines and the mothers pull themselves up straight and fluff out their hair and thrusting their chests forward they gaze at him with wanton desire. He leads his flock inside like the pied piper and only when the door slams behind him does the hormonal horde disperse.

Simone nudges me and quips, "...and breathe."

I look at her and she winks and grins. "Do you know that keeps me going all day until the afternoon repeat. Lordy lord we must have done something

right to deserve such eye candy twice a day."
I smile but don't feel much like laughing and I see the sympathy in her eyes. "Come on doll face let's get you home, we need to sort this mess out."
I nod miserably and gather up my wayward puppy as we go from his tether on the railings as we set off for home.

Chapter Three

I sit down and watch Simone bustling around my kitchen dragging out some coffee mugs and setting the percolator.

She is like a well oiled machine in a crisis as I should know, due to the fact that there is normally one going on in my life most days. Not like this though, this is something else entirely.

Pushing a steaming mug of coffee towards me she grabs the squirty cream and finishes it off with a flourish. "Lots of cream today I think, just what the doctor ordered."

I look at her gratefully and then almost spit it out as I take a sip and burn my tongue in the process. I can feel the cream all around my face and know that my face must be redder than an overripe tomato.

Simone looks at me guiltily. "Oops sorry Sophie, maybe you should have let it cool down a bit first." She grabs me a glass of water and I use it to put out the fire in my mouth.

Simone looks at me with a grim expression. "Now tell me everything. We need to work out how to play this." I shrug. "There's not much to tell. He woke me up this morning and told me that he has met someone else and wants a divorce. Just that, no warning, no nothing. It came completely out of the blue and I never saw it coming."

Simone's eyes narrow. "Another woman you say. Do

we know who she is?"

I shake my head. "No -*WE*- do not. The only thing I can think of is that she works with him, I mean he doesn't go anywhere but work, oh and the golf course." Simone looks thoughtful. "Typical mid life crisis if you ask me. Debbie Dooley had the same thing. As soon as her husband turned forty he grew his hair long and took up the guitar. She had to stop him from ditching his job in favour of life on the road." I nod remembering the story. Gosh the playground mafia dined out on that one for a whole half a term and he didn't actually leave Debbie. I am going to be news for a whole term if not the rest of the school year.

We sit for a moment in silence contemplating what has happened. Mr Tumnus starts chasing a yoghurt pot around the room which brings us both back from our thoughts. Simone suddenly looks at me with a very determined expression.

"I think I saw a film like this once. There was this other woman and the wife stalked her. She found out that her husband was not only seeing her but someone else as well. The three of them got together and paid him back, that is what we must do, seek out this Trollope and spy on her until we have something against her or him and then sister we are bringing them down."

Despite myself I grin. "This isn't a film Simone. I'm sure it's just as he said, he has met someone else and he doesn't want me anymore."

As I say the words a huge sob finds it way out of me and I look at my friend in shock. I have actually forgotten to cry about this. For some reason the emotional part hasn't reached me yet, perhaps it will this afternoon and I will lie on the settee crying into a tub of ice cream like they do on the television."

Simone reaches out and grasps my hand. "Ok what about this then? You find a super hot hunk of a guy that is the leader of the mafia. You agree to be his sex prisoner for six months - longer if you prefer in return for him taking a contract out on Lysander. It's a win win situation."

I laugh almost hysterically. "You've been reading too many New Adult novels again. As if those guys exist in the real world."

Simone grins. "They do in my head darling and they come to life in my dreams."

I brave a sip of the coffee and look at her sadly. "How did it come to this? Poor Harry he will have to face life between two homes and have another woman wanting him to call her mummy. How can I bear it? I will have to share him and I will become one of those women that have to put on a brave face when I see them and not talk about them badly in front of him even though I will want to at every given opportunity. I don't want to share my son and I don't want to share my husband. Why should I?"

Before she can answer the phone rings. We freeze and stare at each other and I whisper, "What if that's him, what do I say?"

Simone looks at me angrily. "Listen to what he has to say and then answer just yes or no. Don't show any emotion because then he has won."

I nod and grab the phone and try to say in a strong voice, "Hello."

My heart lurches as I hear my husband's voice coming through quiet and hesitant. "Are you ok Sophie? I gave you quite a shock earlier, have you had time to think about it?"

Simone looks at me her eyes wide and I just say loudly, "Yes."

There is a short silence and then he says, "Good then it will be best for all involved if we deal with this quickly and amicably. I will come home later and get some of my things. If you have any questions we can discuss them then but it may be best to keep emotion out of it for the time being. I mean we don't want to unsettle Harry do we?"

I can feel the rage boiling within me as he speaks. I picture him in front of me and the scene from Kill Bill when she gouges his heart out comes to mind. As the red mist descends all I can do is say, "No."

I hear his sigh of relief and he says in a perkier voice. "Good, I will see you at 7pm. No need to make me any dinner I will have eaten already. Until then then."

All I can say is, "Yes."

He hangs up leaving me standing here holding the phone in shock. Simone gently takes the phone from my hand and leads me to the settee. "There now, that's the first hurdle over with. What did he say?" I tell her and watch as her eyes widen in shock and disbelief. "Ok change of plan. He is going down and you are not going to make this easy on him. Where are your bin bags?"

I look at her in confusion and she grins wickedly. "Come on we're going to pack for him and when he comes he will find his bags out by the bins where he belongs. You will tell him firmly that he is to discuss everything with you via email from now on and the only person he can speak to is Harry. If he wants out then he's out end of. You are not going to be a pushover and after we have packed his miserable life up into those bags then we are getting you the sharpest divorce lawyer that we can find. You know I think I know just the one."

She laughs at my dazed expression. "You know that footballer's wife that lives in Oxshott? Well she got the lot due to his playing more than a game of football. She's not cheap but the rewards more than compensate for it."

I look at her and shake my head. "Does she do legal aid because the only money I have is in our joint account?" Simone screws up her face in thought. "Probably not but leave it with me. My sister went to school with her; maybe she will do it as a favour to her."

I don't have time to argue before I find myself stuffing Lysander's clothes and worldly goods into a roll of bin bags.

It doesn't take us long and Simone turns to me her

eyes shining. "There let's see how he likes a surprise for once. Now I will have Harry over for a sleep over tonight to keep him out of the way. You can confront lover boy and pretend you're Uma Thurman. Make yourself look super hot and in charge so that he knows that you're not going to be messed around. Don't let him in and certainly don't let him take control. You must gain the upper hand in this and be strong. He will regret the day that he let his dick off the leash."

Chapter Four

So here I am waiting for my errant husband with my insides tied up in knots. True to her word Simone has taken charge of Harry for the night and I have primped and preened myself into the hottest version of myself that I can get. Nervously I fiddle with my hands as I wait for the dreaded hour.

Mr Tumnus starts growling as we hear the car pulling up in the drive. Steeling myself for the impending confrontation I down the glass of red wine in front of me for Dutch courage.

Before he can even get the key in the lock I fling it open and look at him with a hard expression.

He looks at me in shock which then softens as he sees me standing there. "Sophie darling, how are you feeling?"

He makes to push past me but I stand my ground. "Not tonight Lysander, you will find your bags are already packed and waiting for you by the bins. Sorry I couldn't get in the loft to get the suitcases but I actually couldn't be bothered. Now Harry is at a friends and I am on my way out. Anything you have to say please put in an e mail in future. You can call Harry but any further dealings with me must be conducted through my solicitor who will be in touch." As I go to close the door he puts his foot in the way blocking it and looks at me in complete and utter shock. "Sophie this isn't like you. We need to discuss this."

I raise my eyes. "There is nothing to discuss. You want to leave so leave. I am not interested in the details and am only concerned with my son. Like I said the best way we can sort this out is amicably via e mail as far as I'm concerned. You've made your decision so there's not much point in dragging it out." I watch as his eyes narrow and that vein in his neck starts twitching which it does when he gets angry. He splutters, "You bitch. What gives you the right to throw me out like a bag of rubbish? It's no wonder I fell in love with someone else living with a cold bitch like you. You don't get to tell me what's happening I tell you. I pay the bills in this house and you had better treat me with the respect I deserve if you want to come out of this with anything. I will go because I can't bear to look at you a moment longer. If it's a fight you want then bring it on."

He removes his foot and I slam the door, my heart thumping in my chest. Quickly I lock the door and then back away from it and sit down on the stairs. In my mind all I can see is his furious face. He didn't like the fact that I was taking control in the slightest and despite the fact that he is the one in the wrong I can see that I have a battle on my hands.

I can't stop shaking and I can feel the tears welling up inside. I push them down. I will be strong. He is the one who has brought all of this about not me and if he doesn't like it then he only has himself to blame. As if on auto pilot I run a bath. I go through the motions of getting ready for bed and am soon wrapped up in my pyjamas with Mr Tumnus on my knee in front of the television. I am quite annoyed that I didn't have the required tub of ice cream in stock. I actually don't know what to do next and am starting to regret listening to Simone already. She has always been the same. She lives out her life as if it was one of the stories in the trashy novels she reads. But this isn't fiction it's fact and I am going to have to make the best of it for both mine and Harry's sake. One thing I am dreading the most though is telling him that his daddy will be living somewhere else in future.

I must have fallen asleep where I sat because I wake up the next morning feeling extremely disorientated. There is a wet patch on my knee where Mr Tumnus must have dribbled in the night. I wake up and see his little furry face looking at me with total adoration and I pull him close to me and kiss him, the tears finally spilling down my cheeks as I contemplate my new life. He wags his tail and then jumps off barking as the doorbell rings.

As I look over at the clock I can see that it is past 9am already. Racing over I open the door and Simone breezes in armed with several shopping bags. "Morning Sophie, at least it looks as if you managed to get some sleep. Harry and Edward are safely at school and today my darling is the first day of the rest of your life." I look at her in shock and she smiles at me. "I've got some shopping in, loads of banned sugar foods and alcohol. Today is all about over indulging and tomorrow is about getting what you deserve. Now run up and get ready whilst I make us a fry up and then we will talk about our options."

In a daze I leave her to it. Typical Simone. She always takes charge and it is what I love about her the most. No problem is ever too great for her and I am sure that she will get me through this. By the time I get downstairs she is hoovering and I see a lovely bunch of lilies dominating the table.

Looking up she grins. "Right then, breakfast is ready. Sit down and I'll tell you where we're at."

Over the bacon and eggs Simone tells me what she spent the evening doing. Apparently she called her sister who has promised to speak to her friend. She has also gone online and printed out sheets and sheets of papers for me on divorce and the do's and don'ts of it all. My homework is to read through them all before the meeting with the solicitor.

The rest of the morning is spent watching DVDs about cheating men to raise my spirits. Where would we be without our friends?

Chapter Five

It's soon time to pick up the children and Simone looks at me and smiles in encouragement. "Don't worry Soph nobody knows yet so let's just act as if its business as usual." I look at her nervously. "It won't be long though. You know what its like around here, the mafia have a way of sniffing out gossip and other people's misery and when that happens my life will never be the same again."

Simone looks at me with sympathy. She knows that it will all burst around me like an atom bomb when word gets out and even she won't be able to protect me from the stares and whispers. I am about to be the subject of discussion around every coffee morning table and social media group chat for some time to come.

With a heavy heart I follow her to the school. Tears burn behind my eyes as I think about what I am going to say to Harry. I will have to tell him something because he will surely notice that his father is MIA. Maybe I can make up some sort of story that he is on a secret mission and can't live with us for security reasons. I know he could be infiltrating a crime ring and can only come back on the odd occasion when the coast is clear. Various scenarios race around my petrified brain, anything to keep from telling him the actual truth, how can I tell him that Daddy doesn't love Mummy anymore?

The playground is packed as usual and I just smile and nod at various other mums as we weave our way through the masses.

I try to ignore the cries of Mr Tumnus who I have tethered to the railings as I venture into the furthest corner in the playground. The trouble is I attract the eye of the last person I want to see - Annabelle Buckley.

A Donatella Versace look-alike who dresses in leopard print and sports the largest black designer sunglasses known to man. She has long bleached blonde hair and a stick thin figure that borders on anorexic. Most of her days are spent at the gym or in the latest fitness class after which she has her nails done or a spray tan. She is married to a record producer and drives the biggest Range Rover that they make. She is the definite queen bee of the playground and everyone aspires to be included in her closed circle. She has a daughter Daisy who is in Harry's class and an older child Sebastian who is in senior school. I feel her eagle eyes zoning in on me and can only wonder if she knows already. I feel Simone stiffen beside me as she anticipates the attack.

Annabelle prowls over to us and fixes us with a probing look. "Ladies, you are both looking gorgeous as usual."

We smile at her nervously and she smiles at us. I say smile but all the happens is that she raises her mouth and shows us her perfect set of veneers however her eyes remain as cold as ice.

"I'm glad I've seen you both I was hoping to ask you a favour." Now this is unusual. I can't imagine what on earth we can help her with. She carries on.

"I am having a little get together at mine tomorrow morning, just a few of my country club friends and I was wondering if either of you were free."

I can feel the shock radiating from Simone as we look at her with stunned expressions.

Simone recovers first and smiles. "I think we're free why how can we help you?" Donatella smiles. "Oh good. I knew that I would be able to count on you both. You see I need some people to serve the guests with their refreshments. I will obviously be far to busy and your duties would involve handing out drinks and nibbles. You're both absolute lifesavers and I won't forget it. Shall we say 10am? You know where I live."

Before we can reply we hear the noise of chattering females subside and know that the moment we have been waiting for all day is about to happen. The school door opens and all eyes turn to take in the divine sight of Mr Rainford.

Everything else is forgotten as we behold the God in front of us. The children race past him which is almost an inconvenience because it distracts the masses from what they really want. He smiles around him and calls out to a few unruly boys who are play fighting and it is hard for the mum's to take their eyes off of him.

Edward comes rushing up and pulls on Simone's hand. "I'm hungry mummy, can I have some sweets?" Without taking her eyes off of the gorgeous teacher Simone puts her hand into her coat pocket and hands her son a packet of starburst.

Edward runs off in delight as Simone savours every last minute of the time she has left before the school doors close. It takes me a while to realise that Harry hasn't come out and I look around me in surprise. "Where's Harry, have you seen him?"

Dragging her gaze away Simone looks around us. "No, let me ask Edward." She calls him over. "Eddie darling where's Harry?" Edward shrugs. "He went home."

Suddenly I feel as if a hand is gripping my heart and squeezing it tightly. Simone catches my eye and looks at me with a frozen look. I manage to stutter out, "What do you mean Edward; he should be in school with you?" Edward looks at me as if I'm stupid. "His daddy came and took him."

Simone reaches over and grabs me, propping me up against the fence before anyone can see. She whispers urgently, "Now take your time, put a smile on your face and move towards Mr Rainford slowly and surely. Don't let anyone see that there is anything wrong. I'll cover you, now go, go, go."

As if on autopilot I cross the playground and head towards the teacher. A puzzled look flashes across his face as he sees me coming and as I reach him he smiles. "Good afternoon Mrs Bailey. Did you need to see me about something?" I look around me furtively and manage to squeak out, "Where's Harry?"

A puzzled look comes over Mr Rainford's face and he draws me over to the side and says quietly, "Your husband came for him just after lunch. He said that he had a dentist's appointment. There's nothing wrong is there?" I can feel my world spinning out of control as I try every trick in the book not to react to his words. Lysander has taken Harry, my baby boy what am I going to do?

Mr Rainford obviously sees my distress and looks at me with concern. He then says loudly, "Thanks for meeting me Mrs Bailey, if you'll come this way please." I can feel the playground eyes searing into my back as I follow him inside. He shuts the door and then we are alone.

Chapter Six

Mr Rainford leads me into the classroom and pulls out a chair for me to sit on. Unfortunately I forget that the chairs are for elves and almost fall over as I wobble precariously on the edge. Fleetingly I wonder if I will ever dislodge myself from it, maybe I will have to wear it like a snail does its home on its back for ever more.

Mr Rainford looks at me with a worried expression. "I'm sorry Mrs Bailey but has something happened?" I look into his gentle brown eyes that are swimming with concern and I well and truly lose it.

Suddenly I am sobbing, great stomach wrenching cries that make me sound like a wild animal. The tears run down my face which must now be quite red and ugly because I have been told on many occasions that I have an ugly cry.

Mr Rainford now looks alarmed for want of a better word and springs forward offering me a tissue from the box on his desk. "It's ok Mrs Bailey, let it all out." I feel my body shaking with the effects of my crying and try desperately to regain some sort of control. I just about manage to hiccup, "I'm sorry but my husband left me yesterday for another woman and now he has taken Harry."

To his credit Mr Rainford keeps calm despite the fact that he allowed my son be kidnapped from underneath his nose. He must now be worrying about the impending scandal and press intervention but I must say that he appears to be dealing with it rather well.

Instead he brings his little chair over next to me and I notice that like me it appears to be wedged on his back. He puts his arm around my shoulders and I feel him squeezing my shoulder. "There there, it's alright. Harry will be perfectly safe; he is with his father after all. They are probably both at home right now waiting for you and it will all have been a misunderstanding."

As I feel his arm around me I wonder if it is wrong of me to be perversely enjoying myself at this my darkest hour.

This is every playground mother's dream and I am living it right here and now. He is probably right and I am over reacting, Harry will be perfectly safe with Lysander. Knowing him he is just getting me back for bin bag gate.

Not wanting to shatter the moment I emit a few more sobs and am rewarded by more shoulder squeezing action. I wonder if it will be in bad taste to take a selfie of this moment. The sight of this on my snap chat and I would be viral within seconds.

Mr Rainford hands me another tissue and says softly. "Would you like me to get you a cup of tea to help with the shock?" I sniff and look at him gratefully. I am sorry but I must be the worst mother in the world at this moment because tea with Mr Rainford is taking priority over locating my son.

He smiles and pulls the chair from off of his back with a flourish.

"Just wait there and I'll be right back."

He heads off and I think about what has happened. Lysander has taken Harry to punish me for yesterday. One thing that is obvious is that he is showing me that he can make life extremely difficult for me if I don't cooperate. Perhaps I was a bit hasty in playing the wronged wife before I gave him a chance to explain.

Suddenly my phone buzzes and my heart leaps as I see that it is from Lysander. I focus on the text through my tear infested eyes and it reads:

Taken Harry to MacDonald's for tea. Be back at 6pm. Sorry to text rather than email but I thought you might be worried. Maybe we can talk about this like grown ups when I get back.

Mindful of Simone's warning I just reply:

Yes.

Almost immediately my phone buzzes again and I can see that it is from Simone.

I'm still waiting. What's going on in there, do you need me?

Rapidly I text back.

No thank you I'm ok just a misunderstanding. I'll call you later after I've had TEA WITH MR RAINFORD!!!!

I laugh as I see the stream of emojies flooding my phone. It's strange how you can be at your wits end one minute and unbelievably happy the next.

Mr Rainford comes back in balancing two mugs of tea on a celebrations tin. He hands me one with a smile and once again crushes his body into the chair next to me. Opening the tin he offers me a shortbread biscuit and smiles. "One of the perks of the job. Teacher's presents. I've got more tins of biscuits in there than Tescos."
I smile and take the biscuit hoping that I don't leave any crumbs on my face. Ugly crying face with crumbs stuck on my tears is not a good look. He looks at me with concern.
"I'm sorry to hear your news Mrs Bailey, I know that it's not what you want to hear but this happens all the time these days. Harry is young enough for it not to affect him too much and it is how you handle things with him that matter most now." I nod and look at him gratefully and a little bit sheepishly.
"I'm sorry about this Mr Rainford. You must be so embarrassed. The last thing you need is a hysterical mother airing her private life in your playground."
He smiles and I sigh inwardly as I see his eyes

crinkle up at the corners and the pure sexuality shining from his eyes. "You aren't the first and won't be the last that's for sure. If I can be of any help at all you only have to ask. I mean I can keep an eye on Harry and make sure that he is ok at school."

I smile at him and nod. "Thank you I would appreciate that. He doesn't know yet and I'm not sure how we are going to tell him. If I'm honest I still don't think that I've fully taken it in myself. I don't know what the next step is, I mean it's all new to me and I suppose I am trying to just carry on as normal when everything is definitely not."

He smiles and offers me another biscuit. "You must take your time to adjust to things before making any decisions. Let the news sink in and accept any offers of support. I am sure that you are not alone and can count on your friends and family to support you. Don't be afraid to ask for help and before long you will find your path."

I sink back and then regret the movement as the chair wobbles precariously.

I say quietly. "I have Simone but my mother and father live in Spain and I'm an only child. All of my friends are couples that I socialise with with Lysander. I am sure that they won't want to get involved. I don't even have a job because I am a stay at home Mum. To be honest when you look at my life it's pretty sad really that that's all I've got to show for my existence so far."

Mr Rainford frowns. "Come on Mrs Bailey there's a

lot more to you than that. You are more than somebody's wife and mother. Maybe it's time you rediscovered who you really are. Let's start right now." To my surprise he holds his hand out and as I reach out he shakes my hand. "I'm pleased to meet you, my name is Daniel and you are?"

I smile and say, "Sophie, I'm pleased to meet you Daniel." He grins. "Now we are friends. That wasn't so bad was it? By the time you've finished you will have many more."

I laugh and once again wonder if it's in bad taste. Surely I shouldn't be laughing with a super hot teacher over tea and shortbread the day after my husband left me for another woman and then abducted my child.

Once again he grins and then stands up, the chair falling to the floor with a clatter. "Now get yourself home and when your little boy comes through that door give him the biggest smile and the tightest hug. He will need a strong mummy now and that is you Sophie Bailey. I will expect a full update tomorrow, same time same place, now don't be late."

He reaches down and grasps my hand pulling me up. To my extreme embarrassment the chair comes with me and is firmly stuck to my behind. Daniel laughs and punches it so that it joins his in a heap on the floor and grins. "I get a worrying sense of satisfaction every time I do that, do you think that I'm a monster?" I smile sweetly at him. "No that's the last word I would use to describe you. Thank you, I mean

that. You've been so kind and I really appreciate it."
His eyes soften and he smiles gently. "It was a
pleasure Sophie. Remember you're not alone there
are lots of people who are here for you ok?"
I smile and gather up my belongings and leave the
room an awful lot happier than I went in.

Chapter Seven

Simone is waiting for me on the green nearby.
Guiltily I remember Mr Tumnus and am relieved to
see him playing with Edward.
Simone waves me over to the bench that she is sitting
on. "Come on Sophie; spill the beans I want to know
every last detail."
Sitting down next to her I am appalled to find that I
am grinning like a Cheshire cat. "It went really well
actually. Apparently Lysander has taken Harry to
MacDonald's so all is well there, unless you count
the fact that he will now be hyper all evening. Daniel
and I had a nice little chat over tea and biscuits and I
am now on my way home to meet my cheating
husband for a show down."
Simone's eyes are wide and her hand flies to her face.
"DANIEL!!! Oh my god why hasn't my husband left
me and abducted my son? Life is so unfair."
We look at each other and burst out laughing.
Shaking my head I look at my phone to see what
time it is, I am sure that watch sales have dwindled
since the invention of the mobile, I mean its life by
phone now isn't it?
Jumping up I say in alarm. "I must get back and get
ready. They will be here soon and the house is a mess
and so am I. Lysander will be appalled and I don't
want to give him any more ammunition against me as
to why he has gone."

Simone looks at me and frowns.

"Just you listen to yourself Sophie Bailey. You are not at fault here. It is because of him that you are in this position and maybe he just needs to see how it has affected you. You don't apologise to him for anything, if anything he should be the one apologising to you. Let him take you as he finds you and who cares what he thinks?"

I smile at her shakily. "You're right it shouldn't matter and I absolutely hate myself for letting me think that it does. Maybe if I had paid more attention to the little things then he wouldn't have felt the need to go elsewhere. I must shoulder some of the blame because if I was doing my job properly as his wife then I wouldn't be in this position now."

I almost cower in fright as Simone stands up and looks at me furiously.

She stands with her hands on her hips and pokes her finger at me crossly. "Listen to yourself Sophie doormat Bailey. Stop blaming yourself and grow a pair. You have been a fantastic wife and mother to those two boys and none of this and I mean NONE of this is your fault. Now stop trying to make excuses for his obvious mid life crisis and remember you are a strong woman who will come out of this and probably have a happier life as a result. If I hear one more word like that drivel that you have just spouted then I am going to karate kick you into next week. Do I make myself clear?"

I nod miserably and then she charges at me and grips

me tightly to her. "I love you silly girl. Now go on and sort this out however you want to play it. Just remember that I am only down the road and will be there within minutes if you need me." Wiping the tears from my eyes I nod and almost manage a smile before grabbing Mr Tumnus and putting him on his lead.

As I head home I think about what Simone said. I suppose I am subconsciously blaming myself because if I had been a good wife he wouldn't be looking elsewhere. We have been married for twenty years but have only had Harry for six of them. It took us ages to conceive and when I did we both looked on it as a huge blessing.

I used to work in the City at a prominent bank which is where I met Lysander. He was a friend of a friend and we hit it off immediately. I suppose we had a charmed life. We had money and used to spend it on going out and holidays. If we wanted something we had it and life was good to us.

We did everything together and had a great social life. When Harry came along we moved out of London to the country and bought a small cottage in the village. After the hustle and bustle of London it took some adjusting to but it was what we both wanted, to bring up our family in a safe, friendly community where everybody knew everyone else.

It was decided that I would give up work to care for Harry and despite everything I found that I loved my new life. Money was tight because now we only had the one income but everybody struggles when they have children don't they? Something had to give and so nights in replaced nights out and life settled into family life.

What I don't know is - what went so badly wrong?

I am still pondering the situation as I put the key in the door. However before I can even open it the door flies open and Harry races out straight past me to Mr Tumnus and grabs hold of him tightly. "There you are boy, I missed you."

Lysander follows him out and grins. "We know our place in his affections. Obviously the dog comes first." I look at him and just nod. I am not in the mood to joke around with him in this way, he has hurt me and my family and until things work themselves out one way or another then any pleasantries will have to wait.

Instead I just turn to Harry and bending down envelop him in a big hug. "Did you have a nice time baby boy?" He grins and pulls me into the house. "They had a play area and I was really good. I went down the scariest slide into the ball pit and it was really great."

I smile. "Did you have a nice tea?" He nods vigorously. "I had a Happy Meal and there was a really cool Pokemon toy in it. Charlie Dawson has it already and now I do too."

Lysander laughs and grabs hold of him and throws him in the air until he screams with excitement.

Ignoring the happy father, son bonding moment I push past them and put my bag and coat away.

I hear Harry shout, "Dad can I play on the Xbox?" Lysander replies, "Go on then twenty minutes tops whilst I speak to mummy."

My heart drops as he comes into the kitchen and closes the door behind him. He leans against it and looks at me with a worried expression.

"How are you Sophie? I'm sorry it must have been quite a shock." I nod not really knowing what to say, I mean if life was like one of Simone's movies or books I would have something quick witted or emotional to say, instead all I can do is shake my head.

So I just look at him and say, "I'm sorry Lysander but I don't really know what to say. I never knew you were unhappy and this has come as a bolt out of the blue. I suppose I am in shock really because I don't think it has sunk in yet."

He looks at me guiltily and shrugs. "The truth is I have felt like this for a long time. Things were all fine until we moved here then life just changed. I was no longer your priority and slipped even further down the list when Mr Tumnus came along. You were preoccupied with Harry and the other mum's and their children. You didn't give me the same attention anymore and I always felt as if being with me was a chore. I would work, come home and then eat my dinner and we would go to bed. You were always tired and even at the weekends all I had was a long list of jobs to do in the house or garden. None of this is what I thought it would be and it took what happened at the doctors to bring it all to a head."

I look at him in surprise. "Why what happened?" He shakes his head. "It was about six months ago that I went because I hadn't been feeling well. The doctors tested me and came to the conclusion that I had anxiety. They recommended a place in town that might be able to help with my stress levels along a more natural route because as you know I am anti drugs. Well when I met Wanda she sort of changed my life. Suddenly I was looking at things through new eyes and I didn't like what I saw. I'm afraid I moved away from you and our life mentally a lot sooner than I am doing physically. I thought that it would go away but if anything it has grown stronger and now it is painfully obvious to me that this is not what I want anymore. Don't get me wrong I still love you and Harry, of course I do but I have to put myself first now because Wanda has taught me that if I am happy then everyone close to me will be happy too."

He smiles at me and squeezes my hand. "I know it's a shock darling but you will soon see that what I am doing is for all of our good. You will thank me for this one day."

I suppose I must be in shock because all I can think of is the scene in Kill Bill when she massacres a room full of people. If I had a samurai sword now I would be unstoppable. Lysander just shakes his head sadly. "Anyway I wanted to explain and to say that I will make this as easy for everyone as I can. You can stay here until the house is sold and then we will split the proceeds and both buy a flat or something. I will arrange the child maintenance and have Harry every other weekend. Don't you worry about a thing because I have worked everything out."

I'm sorry but am I in a parallel universe or something? Lysander seems to think that all of this is as easy as moving house.

I can feel the anger growing inside me and I manage to stutter, "What about Harry, what are you going to tell him?"

Lysander smiles happily. "Oh he's fine about it. I told him when we went to MacDonald's and he is excited to be like some boy called Robbie Barnes who has two families which means two lots of presents at Christmas and birthdays. He's excited to have a second bedroom and actually can't wait to come and visit."

That is it, the icing on the cake, the straw that broke the camel's back and the end of the line. Nothing can stop the rage that is building within me as I listen to him. It's like he is a different person and I don't recognise the man standing in front of me. I don't know what comes over me but all of a sudden I take a swing and punch him right in the face.

My fist throbs painfully as I watch with relish my despicable, errant husband of twenty years fall back across the room clutching his nose as the blood spurts out of it with complete and utter shock on his face.

I look at him my hands on hips Uma Thurman style and say through gritted teeth. "Now get out before I do any more damage. How dare you tell Harry without talking to me first. You think it's all sorted out well let me tell you buster it's far from being over. Like I said before you will hear from my solicitor and if you think this is going to be easy then think again."

I stand back and open the back door as wide as I can. "Now get the Hell out of here back to Wanda who will no doubt have some sort of alternative non drug like potion to patch you up with and never, ever take my child again before clearing it with me first."

Lysander looks at me and his face is almost aubergine purple as he looks at me in anger.

"You total bitch. No more Mr nice guy then. Two can play at this game and you will soon find out that I am rather good at it. Tell Harry I'll call him."

He races out of the door as I slam it shut behind him.

Chapter Eight

"Oh my GOD!!!" Simone is laughing so hard that I think she will burst. "I would love to have seen that." I shake my head glumly. "It's not funny, I shouldn't have done that but he wound me up so much, I mean I could cope with the fact that his reasons were selfish and that all he was concerned about was himself but to tell Harry without discussing it with me first not to mention the fact that he took him out of school to tell him without letting me know, well I just saw red."

Simone puts a sympathetic arm around my shoulder. "It's done now, no point dwelling on it. What's the plan now?"

I look at the school playground that is looming in front of us. "Well I suppose first things first we must get these two off to school, walk Mr Tumnus and then head off to Annabelle, Donatella, Buckley's country club soiree."

Simone winces. "I've been dreading this. The only thing keeping me going is that I get to have a nosey around her home. That will be worth all the tea in china." I nod in agreement.

Harry and Edward race into the playground and my heart sinks as I see Annabelle wave us over. As we reach her she looks at me with interest. "Everything ok Sophie?"

I stiffen up. Innocent enough words but loaded with

potential cluster bomb damage. I smile sweetly. "Fine thank you Annabelle. Are you all set for this morning?" She continues to stare at me and I will myself not to fidget or blush. Then she nods. "Yes meet me at mine at 10am and I will show you what to do. Thanks for helping me out."

I am spared from any more scrutiny as the hallowed classroom door opens and all eyes turn to behold the delicious figure of Mr Rainford.

Simone nudges me and we stare at him with wonder alongside every other mother in the playground. As I look at him I feel a strange smugness that I can call him Daniel and had tea with him yesterday. I almost feel as if it has transcended to the level of an illicit affair and it is as if we have a secret connection because of it.

In my mind I see him approaching me across the crowded playground. In full view of everyone he would pull me towards him and lean down and kiss me gently and then with more passion as the playground mafia look on in jealous awe.

My dream is shattered as the door slams shut and Simone nudges me, "Come on then I'll pick you up just before ten."

Just after 10.00am we find ourselves outside the regency mansion that is home to the head of the yummy mummy brigade. We are silent as we take in the grandeur of the house in front of us. Regency style pillars guard the entrance in front of which stand to attention the obligatory topiary. With a deep breath we ring the bell and stand silently contemplating our fate.

The door is soon opened and we behold the sight of the mistress of the house. Looking like she has just stepped out of a Chanel advert is Annabelle Buckley. She is dressed head to toe in black sporting a Chanel scarf around her neck and wearing heavy expensive looking jewellery. She looks every inch the wealthy wife of a record producer and waves us in with urgency. "Come through ladies, if you follow me to the kitchen I will show you what's what."

We follow in silence not wanting to miss a single minute of gawping at the inside of this house. Despite its grand facade I am happy to report that it is in severe need of an overhaul. It looks as if it hasn't been decorated in years and the threadbare rug in the hallway looks as if it came with the house when it was built. The wallpaper is distinctly 70's chic and the gold ornate mirror on the wall looks in dire need of a dust.

We follow her through into a surprisingly small kitchen that like the hallway is in need of modernisation. I can sense Simone's surprise and daren't catch her eye.

Annabelle stops by a pine dresser and grabs two rolled up aprons off the side and thrusts them at us. "If you could put these on and when the guests arrive show them into the drawing room and then arrange to hand out the hors doevres. You will find them in the fridge and the silver platters in the dresser. I have Champagne in the fridge and soft drinks if they prefer. However knowing this lot they will drink my cellar dry."

She laughs as if she is the most hysterical person on earth and we just smile politely. She looks around and says briskly, "Good, I'll leave you to it then. I will be in the drawing room if you need me."

As soon as she goes Simone grins. "Well it's all been worth it. Who'd have thought that Annabelle, I have it all, Buckley lives in a crumbling pig sty." I laugh and then feel a bit bad. "It's not so bad Simone. I mean this place is huge and the furnishings are probably all antiques." Simone laughs. "It looks like this place could do with a good scrub. I bet she does no housework at all, it's probably beneath her." I laugh and then look around me. "Come on let's get to it. First stop the fridge."

Once again we try to contain our laughter as we take in the sight of the Tesco's Value party food all stuffed in the fridge fighting with each other for space. One by one we unwrap the sausage rolls, scotch eggs and mini quiches and arrange them on the silver platters. Simone giggles. "I wonder what her guests would say if they saw what they were eating. I bet she pretends it's from Waitrose, or caterers." I laugh as I grab some glasses from the dresser. "I think these need a good wipe as well. I can feel the dust on them."

Simone and I set to work cleaning the glasses and

then filling them with the cheapest Prosecco that I know is on offer at Tesco's. Gosh how the other half live!

Chapter Nine

It doesn't take long before the doorbell rings and Simone looks at me and pulls a face. Do you want to go first or shall I?

I grin. "I'll go; it will take my mind off how much of a mess my life is in at the moment." Simone looks at me sympathetically but I just shrug and go to answer the door.

There are two ladies looking every inch as glamorous as Annabelle and they just walk on past me as if I don't exist, thrusting their coats at me as they go. They seem to know where they are going so I just leave them to it and put their coats in a cupboard under the stairs that appears to be the place for them. Simone meets me on her way out with the champagne and rolls her eyes. "The things we find ourselves roped into."

It doesn't take long for the rest to arrive and I am actually quite glad of the distraction. There is only so much washing and ironing that I can do whilst dwelling on my broken heart. Despite how Lysander has been I still love him, I can't just switch off twenty years of what I thought was a happy marriage like he obviously can.

Luckily I am kept busy and am surprised when the doorbell rings about an hour later. Simone is handing out the mini quiches so I go to answer the door.

A pleasant looking woman is standing there and

looks surprised when I answer. "Oh I'm sorry I don't think we've met before, my name is Frances and you are?"

I smile. "Sophie, I'm pleased to meet you."

She smiles and then raises her eyes as she takes in my apron. "So you've been roped into playing maid for lady muck have you? Well I hope she's paying you well."

I smile. "Oh no it's just a favour to help her out."

Frances pulls a face. "Hmm I bet you didn't have much choice in the matter. Never mind lead me into the fray if you will."

I laugh and walk with her to the drawing room. The shrieks of laughter bouncing from the walls makes her wince and she looks at me in desperation. "I hope there's some strong stuff in there because I think I'm going to need it."

Before I can reply Annabelle sees her and shrieks, "Frances how good of you to come."

I watch with amusement as she proceeds to air kiss Frances three times with a great show of affection and I see the looks of awe on the faces of her other guests. Obviously Frances is the guest of honour and I can only wonder who she is.

I head back to the kitchen and help Simone re-fill some glasses.

"Ever wondered how the other half live Sophie?"

I grin. "I never thought it would be like this. I think I prefer my life than hers - I mean what's the point of having money and status if you're like those people.

Doesn't seem like much fun does it?"

We hear laughing from the doorway and look around us guiltily.

Frances comes into the room and grins. "You've got the measure of them. I so need a cigarette but everywhere is non smoking these days and I hoped to find the exit through here." Simone smiles. "It's just through there. Would you like to take some champagne with you?" Frances laughs. "If that's champagne then I'm Victoria Beckham. Do you know what I'd really love?" We shake our heads as she smiles. "A really strong cup of coffee."

Simone laughs. "Coming right up, how many sugars?" Frances grins. "Two but don't tell anyone, especially that lot in there, I wouldn't hear the end of it for months. They are all on a strictly low fat, no carbs, lettuce and champagne diet and would be horrified to learn that I stuffed two whole Krispy Cremes down my throat before I came."

We laugh and Frances looks at us with interest. "So tell me how do you know Annabelle?"

I roll my eyes. "From the playground. Our children go to the same school." Frances nods. "Oh I see. It would appear that the bullies grow up into bullies as adults, I bet you daren't say no to her kind offer of servitude."

Simone grins. "You've got it in one. How did you guess?"

Frances smiles and pulls out a chair and sits down beckoning us to follow suit. "Oh I've got the measure of Annabelle and people like her. I see them every day and the country club is crawling with them. Like you I have been bullied into coming here today because I didn't want to get in her bad books."

Simone looks surprised. "You don't seem the type to worry about what people say if you don't mind me saying Frances."

She smiles ruefully. "Ordinarily no but I have resisted her too many times to think up a plausible enough reason to turn her down again. I just thought that I'd get it over with and then she can stop hounding me. I only go to the club for the gym and the bar. My husband and I like to unwind there after a hard day sometimes and it is difficult to avoid the country club mafia as I call them as they are always there holding court."

As she talks about her husband my eyes fill up with tears and she looks at me sharply. "Are you ok Sophie?"

I sniff as Simone reaches over and takes my hand. "Sophie's two timing cheat of a husband has just left her and her son for another woman and sprung it on her when she didn't even know anything was wrong. He also kidnapped her son and took him to MacDonald's and told him behind her back."

Frances looks shocked and Simone grins. "It's ok though because she punched him and threw him out."

The tears start falling and Frances looks shocked. "What a despicable thing to happen. He certainly deserved the punch but you probably shouldn't have done that because he will no doubt have photographed his face as evidence in your divorce hearing."

I look at her in confusion and she smiles softly. "Don't worry I'm sure it will be fine. Men are such bastards aren't they?"

I sniff. "The trouble is I didn't see it coming. I thought we were happy. I mean I have always tried to follow the Jerry Hall principles of marriage. Be a cook in the kitchen, a maid in the living room and a whore in the bedroom. The trouble is by the time I did the first two I was so shattered there wasn't time for the whore part, not to mention the fact that Lysander likes to get to November before putting the heating on so I wrap up in multiple layers of fleece at bedtime which he always moaned about. How was I to know this would happen?"

Frances and Simone nod their heads in agreement. Simone looks at me with sympathy. "It was the same for me until I read Fifty Shades. The genius move was getting Martin to read it too, well that certainly lit the touch paper and our lives haven't been the same since. If you saw the images on my kindle book covers you would think that you had wandered into a porn shop. I've had to set it to covers off just in case Edward gets hold of it. You can hide a lot of smut behind a Cath Kidston kindle cover."

Frances nods. "It's true. I've read it too and it changed my life for the better. I'm never without my kindle now, it's my female Viagra."

Despite myself I burst out laughing. "How did I not know this? I must be the only woman alive who doesn't know about this new sexual revolution." Simone smirks. "I have been trying to tell you. Don't say I haven't."

Suddenly we notice the time and Simone jumps up in alarm. "I had better get the mini cheese balls out of their packaging and throw them to the animals. The last thing we need is our leader descending on us in full battle mode." I nod and reluctantly push back my chair. Frances looks at me and smiles. "Chin up Sophie, you will be fine don't worry. Just get yourself a good divorce lawyer and make sure that you get what you deserve."

I look at her sadly. "I'm not sure that will be possible Frances. You see I gave up work years ago when we had Harry. I have no money only what Lysander gives me for housekeeping. Solicitors aren't cheap so I will just have to agree to whatever Lysander says. Hopefully he will see us alright; I mean he's not that bad really."

Frances looks at me and narrows her eyes. "Don't you believe that Sophie, if he wasn't so bad then you wouldn't be finding all this out now. Is there anybody you can ask to help you?"

Simone looks over and her face hardens. "My sister is going to ask her old school friend Mimi Constable, she might owe her a favour or something and then Sophie's cheating husband will get what's coming to him."

Frances looks impressed. "Wow she's the best. I wouldn't want her coming after me. Do you think you stand a chance at her agreeing, I mean she's not cheap?" Simone grins. "I think we stand a very good chance."

I look at her in surprise. "What makes you say that?" Simone laughs. "Well my sister is the admin officer for The Duchess of Cornwall private school; you know the one that everyone has to go to around here. Well places are like gold dust and I happen to know that Mimi's daughter Imogen is on the reserve list. My sister told me that she would be calling her today with an offer she won't be able to refuse. My bet is by this afternoon you will have your lawyer and it won't cost you a penny."

Frances laughs out loud and my eyes fill up once again. "Do you really think she will say yes?" Frances grins. "Of course she will. It will be a small price for her to pay to ensure her daughter's future. Genius move if you ask me."

Simone grins. "It's not what you know but who you know and Lysander is going to find out that you now know some very formidable people. By the time she's finished he will rue the day that he ever ventured into that alternative life."

We are interrupted as we hear footsteps approaching from down the hall. Quickly we make ourselves look busy as Annabelle bursts into the room.

She sees Frances and pastes a sugary grin on her face. "Oh Frances there you are. I hope that Simone

and Sophie haven't been boring you with life as a stay at home mummy, why don't you come back with me, the girls were wondering where you are?"
I see a look of desperation flash across Frances's face and stifle a giggle as Annabelle leads her reluctantly out of the room.

Chapter Ten

The rest of the morning flashes past and by the time we have tidied up it is time to go and collect the boys from school.

As we go to leave Annabelle flashes us what she calls a smile and says, "Thanks ladies I owe you one. I think that it went well don't you? Anyway you know you should really consider joining the Country club, you meet such interesting people there and it expands your horizons past the school gate. Have a word with your husbands, I am sure they will only be too happy to pay for it, I mean a happy wife is a willing wife after all."

Simone looks at her and narrows her eyes as mine once again fill with tears.

Simone fixes her with a hard look. "Thanks Annabelle we may consider it but if I'm honest with you I doubt that I would be able to fit it in. I mean what with my tennis lessons, Pilate's classes and Latin degree I am not sure that I would find the time."

Annabelle looks surprised. "Gosh Simone why on earth are you wasting time learning Latin? You don't need to be doing that when you have a husband to look after you, surely it's all about enjoying yourself whilst you are still young enough to?"

Simone shrugs. "You'd learn Latin if you saw who teaches it. Mr Rainford has nothing on Emilio. If I didn't get my weekly fix of him then I would be unbearable."

Annabelle looks interested and then turns to me. "What about you Sophie shall I put your name down?"

I look down and shake my head trying to think up a good excuse. Simone pipes up, "I doubt that Sophie can manage it either what with her new business and all." I look up in surprise and see Annabelle looking interested. "What is it Sophie, you're a dark horse aren't you?" I look at Simone in desperation and she grins. "Sorry Annabelle we can't say at the moment because it's a secret. Don't worry though you will be the first to know."

Before Annabelle can say any more Simone grabs my arm and pulls me through the rather large front door.

We jump in the car and I look at Simone and laugh. "So what's my big business then?" Simone grins. "Who knows but it will be eating her up. She will now want to know what it is so badly; it may be fun playing with her for a bit. Also it's the perfect excuse to use to get out of playing servant to her at her next soiree. I need a shower to wash off the dust from that mausoleum, worth it though, I will always have it in the back of my mind when she tries to lord it over me in the playground in the future."

I have to agree with her. It was certainly a surprise seeing Annabelle's house. It's funny how you form impressions of people just by their appearance. I always thought that Annabelle lived in modern chic luxury with all the latest mod cons. I would never have pictured her in that crumbling dust palace.

Soon we join the rest of the mafia in the playground and it doesn't take long before the bell rings and we all gaze expectantly towards the door.

A hush descends on the playground as it opens and Mr Rainford leads his charges out to be reclaimed by their doting mothers. I hold my breath along with every other mother here who all drink in every last perfect drop of his face and body to sustain them through the night.

I almost forget about Harry until his loud voice rings out. "Mummy, Daddy says that I can go to his new house and choose the wallpaper for my room, can I pleeease. I want it to be a Transformers room. Josh Evans has it and Daddy did say that I could choose whatever I wanted."

I feel the eyes of every mother here swing sharply over to my direction. The silence is palpable and I feel Simone stiffen up in shock beside me. It is as though Harry has dropped an Atom bomb in the playground and the fallout will be every bit as devastating.

I am frozen to the spot and feel my mind spinning out of control. I almost can't breathe and daren't look at anyone, this is it, my secret is out and life will never be the same again. I am now officially gossip that will feed these mothers for the next year.

Once again the tears threaten to fall but before I can speak I hear one voice ringing out across the playground offering me an extremely welcome lifeline.

"Mrs Bailey, can I have a word please?" The eyes all swing away from me back to the source of the oasis. Mr Rainford is looking at me and smiling the most toe curling, sexy, take me here and now in the playground sort of smile and I feel Sophie push me forward as she whispers, "I've got this, I'll look after Harry now get the hell out of here."

I walk as if in a trance towards my saviour as I feel the laser stares of the mafia. I am just about aware of the fact that Mr Rainford is holding the door open for me as I reach my sanctuary.

I hear the door close behind us and then there is silence. Mr Rainford takes my arm and gently propels me towards the classroom. "Come on Sophie, I'll put the kettle on and you can hide out here until the crowd disperses."

Once again I sit down into the little plastic cocoon that snaps around my body as I try to gather myself together. That's it my secret is out; no more pretending this is now as real as it gets. Single, soon to be divorced mother of one and a dog taking on the world and struggling to find her way. I have never felt as alone as I do now.

Suddenly a mug is pushed into my hands and I look up into the gorgeous eyes of my saviour who is looking at me with concern.

"Here drink this Sophie, I have put in extra sugar for energy and we are on the bourbons today so help yourself." I try to smile but the tears fall down my cheeks instead. Daniel smiles and hands me a tissue saying softly, "Take your time Sophie; you know it's not all that bad. It had to come out at some point and at least everyone found out at the same time. Now they know and you can move on."

I look down and watch as a tear splashes into my tea. I sniff and say softly, "The trouble is I'm still trying to get my head around it myself. Things are moving so quickly and I haven't had time to adjust to it. Harry doesn't really understand what it all means and I suppose neither do I."

Daniel reaches over and takes the mug from my hands and places it on the gnome sized table beside us. To my surprise he pulls me towards him and just holds me gently rubbing my back. For a moment I am in shock. I am in Daniel's arms and I never want to leave. I have dreamed of this moment along with every last mother in the playground. Who would have thought it would be as easy as having your husband leave you and destroy your life in the process to get your heart's desire?

I can hear his heart beating in the silence around us as he continues to stroke my back. I savour the feeling of comfort and then to my utter dismay huge sobs flow from my body and the tears rain down like Niagara Falls. Suddenly the floodgates open and I cannot close them. I sob uncontrollably in Daniel's arms for the life I used to have. I cry for the past, present and future and it all flashes through my mind at once. Suddenly it is just me Sophie Bailey against the world and it is a frightening place.

Chapter Eleven

To be honest I am not sure how long we sit here for. Perversely I am enjoying the complete breakdown that I am now going through and intend on milking it for all it is worth. Opportunities don't come along every day like this and I fully intend on making the most of it.

Every time I think that I am ok I feel another little comforting rub on my back and I am sorry to say that I utter another small sob just to prolong the encounter. If I could video this moment I would and put it on repeat every hour of the day.

However I suddenly remember that I have a child and a dog to see to and reluctantly pull away.

Daniel looks at me and smiles softly and I drink in every last drop of his perfect face.

"That's better Sophie, you needed that. Now you've got that out of you things won't be so bad." I sniff and to my complete mortification honk loudly into the tissue.

He hands me another one and smiles. "Harry will be fine. Children adapt very quickly to things and soon he won't know any different. The person that worries me the most though is you. Is there anyone who you can count on for support?"

I shake my head. "Only Simone. My parents live in Spain and I'm an only child. To be honest I don't really have a plan. I suppose I will have to work one out quickly though because things will need to change. I suppose I will have to get a job and my husband has said that he wants to sell the house and split the proceeds. I don't have any money of my own so how I will afford to pay a mortgage is beyond me."

Daniel looks at me sympathetically.

"It's a mess that's for sure. I wouldn't worry though, I'm a great believer in fate and something is telling me that you will be ok. You know you could always work here for a bit until you get yourself sorted. It might also be a distraction for you."

Suddenly the shock I felt when Lysander delivered his shocking blow pales into insignificance at the shock that I am now feeling. Work here with Daniel? Now I know there's a God. I look at him in surprise and he grins.

"The fact is we need some help here at the school. Mrs Fletcher is retiring next month and we need a replacement. If you would consider it I would be happy to give you the job. You could work around Harry and although the money isn't much it will help out a bit and it may distract you from your current situation and give you something else to think about."

Once again the tears fill my eyes and Daniel smiles. "Its not that bad is it? I mean working with me." I smile and a small laugh escapes. "No I think that I could handle it. But you are being so kind I suppose I'm not used to it at the moment."

Handing me another tissue Daniel smiles and I notice how his eyes twinkle. "Maybe you should hold that thought Sophie Bailey because you may not think so after a few weeks working with me. For all you know I could be a tyrant and you will have my photo up on a dart board quicker than you can shout bulls eye." I laugh and his face softens. "That's better. See it's not all bad. You will get through this you know." As I look into his kind gentle eyes I suddenly have a feeling that he is right, fate does work in mysterious ways and suddenly there is a future for me out there. It may be a different one to the one I had last week, but all the same it is my future, mine and Harry's and I will not let him down. No, it's time to re-discover myself and take charge of my own destiny and it might as well start right here and now working for this gorgeous man in front of me.

"YOU ARE KIDDING ME!!" I have to laugh as Simone looks at me in complete and utter shock. She shakes her head. "I can't believe it you are so lucky Soph. You know my bet is by the end of the first week he will have had his way with you on every desk in that school not to mention the stationery cupboard." I feel my shoulders shaking as I laugh uncontrollably, possibly with a mix of hysteria. "Don't be ridiculous Simone. You've still got your head in one of your books. This is the real world and it's just an admin job at the local school. Anyway I've told you before I think he's gay."

Simone snorts. "Keep telling yourself that Sophie.
No I think its all part of his master plan. He has seen
you and desired you for months. Somehow he has
engineered this whole thing and paid this woman to
seduce Lysander so that he could get you where he
wants you, right between his sex God legs." I can't
even speak for the now mad and slightly psychotic
laughter that is wracking my body.

Simone came back to mine after I finally made it out
of the classroom for a full debrief. The children are
playing with Mr Tumnus on the trampoline in the
garden and we have cracked open a bottle of Pinot
Grigio to celebrate my new working status.

Simone grins. "Wait until the mafia hear about this
latest development. Annabelle Buckley will think
this is the business that I spoke about so it has all
worked out rather well wouldn't you say?"

I grin at her. "You must be a witch. You must have
seen this coming in your crystal ball." Simone
cackles evilly. "One more thing I can see in your
future is lots of hardcore sex with a certain teacher
not far from here. He won't be able to keep his hands
off you and you will become his sex slave."

I snort into my wine. "For god's sake Simone read
War and Peace or something and give us all a rest.
I'm sure that he has a boyfriend and when I find out
you will have to think up some other fantasy that you
have for me."

Simone suddenly looks excited. "You know what
Sophie, things have moved on a lot since we were

young, free and single. You must register with an online dating site; God only knows how much sex is out there for the taking. You could have a different one every week."

I shake my head and roll my eyes. "Calm down Simone. The last thing I am doing is registering myself on a dating site. They are full of weirdoes and are probably all married men on there anyway looking for kicks. No there are only two men in my life now and they are bouncing around outside on the trampoline."

As I say it I look out and feel slightly concerned as I see Mr Tumnus bouncing higher than the boys as they stamp on the trampoline to see how high he can go. I move over to the door and race over and manage to catch my furry friend as he bounces off. I really should have bought the trampoline with the safety net attachment. Will I ever stop feeling the guilt of bad parenting?

Chapter Twelve

"I'm not sure that this is such a good idea Simone." I
look at my friend with a worried expression. It was
all her idea that seemed like a good one at the time
after downing the bottle of wine last night, but now
in the cold light of day as I look up at the sign,
"Wanda's Alternative World" it seems like a very bad
one indeed.

Simone had decided that we need to find out more
about this other woman and has devised a plan to
infiltrate the enemy camp on a fact finding mission. I
am not sure that it was completely necessary to dress
all in black for the occasion and wear the dark
sunglasses but in my emotional state I would wear a
wedding dress if she told me to.

Simone looks at me with a grim expression.

"We have to do this Sophie and remember don't tell
her who we are. We need to have the element of
surprise on our side. All we are is two normal
housewives looking for a pick me up; remember the
story and we will make it out alive."

I look at her and nod miserably. If I'm honest I don't
feel ready to meet the woman who has stolen my
hopes and dreams for the future. What if I am
overwhelmed with rage and karate chop her to death.
I will be incarcerated for murder and my dream of
the perfect life with Daniel would be over. Ever since
I found about the job I have been having the most

amazing fantasies about life with Daniel. Simone's description is nothing compared to the X rated dreams I have been having and I am not sure that I will be able to face him at all now after what I have imagined him doing to me.

However nothing gets in Simone's way when she has set her mind to it and my heart sinks as I follow her inside the shop.

The stench of joss sticks is the first thing that my brain registers which makes me want to heave even more than I did outside. As I look around me I take in the sight of crystals and dream catchers hanging from the ceiling and shelves groaning under the weight of self help and therapy books.

Looking around I see the various potions and creams residing on Ikea bookcases and there is a strange sort of whale music playing all around us.

I catch Simone's eye and she looks at me with determination. Suddenly I am aware that someone has come out from behind a beaded curtain and quickly avert my eyes. I hang back and pretend to be engrossed in a book on making your own medicine as I am not sure that I am ready to face the woman who has detonated the bomb that has exploded my life.

I hear a soft voice wafting across the shop towards me saying, "Good morning is there anything I can help you with?" Strangely her voice draws me in and I raise my eyes to take in the sight of the woman who has stolen my heart.

My breath catches in my throat and I look at Simone in bewilderment. She looks at me with total shock because quite frankly Wanda, if that is who this woman is, is nothing at all like I thought she'd be. Standing behind the counter is a rather large woman wearing a pink and green caftan. Her hair explodes crazily out of her head and is of the softest grey. She must be at least sixty due to her lined face and her eyes regard us kindly as she smiles at us welcomingly.

Simone recovers first and coughs nervously. "Umm you might be able to help me. I was wondering if you had a sort of pick me up. I am feeling tired and drained of energy and subsequently feel a bit stressed."

Wanda nods in understanding. "Yes life is so full on these days it doesn't surprise me. I do have something that might help you but it will be a quick fix. What you really need is to change your lifestyle; you know routine, eating habits that sort of thing." She looks at Simone thoughtfully. "I think that I could help you. You know I run classes in lifestyle changes and my students all swear by them. I have some details here if you're interested."

She hands Simone a leaflet and then turns to look at me. Suddenly I am looking into the eyes of the woman who has stolen my husband, I think, and to say I'm shocked is an understatement.

She looks at me kindly. "What about you dear. You

look like you could use a pick me up if you don't mind me saying so. I can tell you know, it's in your aura."

Simone looks interested. "Can you really see her aura? - cool." Wanda nods. "Yes I have a certain gift and I can tell that something has greatly saddened your friend. Maybe I can help you both re discover your energy and strengthen your aura."

She rummages behind her on the shelf and Simone looks at me incredulously. I watch as Wanda thrusts something towards us that looks like cake.

"Here try a sample. This is full of natural pick me ups. It has healing qualities that are completely organic. I sell it in cake form for my young ladies as you can eat a slice of it with your morning elevenses. Much more civilised than popping a pill every day wouldn't you agree?" I move over to the counter and join Simone as we help ourselves to the drug infested cake. Wanda smiles. "Let me get you both a nice cup of herbal tea. That should lift your spirits and with the cake it will start the healing process almost immediately."

Without waiting for a reply she disappears into the back and I watch in disbelief as Simone crams as much cake into her mouth as possible.

"Oh this is so good Soph; I must buy a whole load of it. I wonder what's in it."

I frown and then she suddenly realises why we are here and whispers. "We may as well get what we can out of the witch. I am not leaving until I find out everything I can about her. I mean she might be some sort of drug pusher or something and then we can shop her to the feds and she will go down for life and become someone's bitch in prison."

I look at her sternly. "This isn't Miami Vice you know. Come on Simone let's get out of here, this doesn't feel right." The trouble is before we can make our escape witch Wanda comes back bearing three mugs of a steaming brew.

She hands us one each and as I take it the scent of peppermint hits me. Wanda smiles gently. "Here you go ladies. If you like it I can sell you some. It's best to replace your normal brand with this and let me tell you when you start on it there's no going back."

I am now very worried about the narcotic nature of what she is feeding us. For all we know she could have laced all of this with hard drugs and we will become addicts and hound her shop for a fix every day. What if that is what happened with Lysander? He might be drugged up to his eyeballs- that would certainly explain his new life choice. I mean it is bad enough that I have lost him to another woman but quite frankly I never expected her to be as old as his mother. If I'm honest I am now feeling even more put out than if she had been a supermodel. I mean what on earth does that say about me?

I am suddenly aware of Simone chattering excitedly with Wanda. She is asking lots of questions and they are getting on like a house on fire. As I frown Wanda looks over and smiles. "Sorry girls I never introduced myself. I'm Wanda and you are?" I look at Simone in alarm and she quickly says, "I'm Chantelle and this is Winona." She shrugs as I look at her incredulously and Wanda smiles warmly. "What lovely interesting names. So tell me about yourselves." Simone gets that look in her eye that spells trouble and I sigh inwardly and brace myself for what is coming.

I hold my breath as Wanda looks at us. Simone frowns and gesturing towards me says, "The reason that my friend's aura is corrupted is because her slime ball of a husband has decided to ditch her and their son after twenty years of marriage for some tart that he met whilst he was in the throws of a full blown mid life crisis."
She looks at Wanda with a hard expression and I look anywhere but at the two of them. I feel so awkward and the silence is now palpable.
Wanda looks over and I feel her eyes boring into me. To my surprise she comes around from behind the counter and stands before me. I look at her face and she is looking at me with such compassion that I feel strangely wrong footed. "I'm so sorry my dear, what a terrible thing to have happened. No wonder you have such sadness, and a young child as well. How old is he?"
I look at Simone whose face is set and just mumble, "He's six years old." To my surprise Wanda's eyes mist over and she grabs hold of me and pulls me to her and hugs me tightly. Now this is an odd situation.

I am now being comforted by my husband's new lover who is sympathising with me for my loss. I am smothered by the scent of Anais Anais, I recognise it because that is what my mother used to use when I was growing up.

I almost can't breathe and wonder fleetingly if she intends to smother me to conveniently get me out of the picture.

Oddly I find the hug quite comforting and just for a moment I relax against her as she whispers, "There there, everything will be ok."

As I pull back I look over at Simone who is looking at us with interest. Wanda smiles kindly. "This is not the first time that I have heard this story." I tense up waiting to hear what she means. Is she about to tell me what I need to know?" She stares at me and for some reason I want her to hug me again, don't ask me why but it felt…well nice actually.

She smiles gently. "Whoever this man is he has done you a huge favour in the long run. It obviously wasn't meant to be and despite the fact that it hurts now you will soon heal and move on. He was obviously not your soul mate and now you have been released to seek him out."

Why does an image of Daniel suddenly fill my mind? Maybe it is him, my soul mate as Wanda puts it. Gosh I suddenly feel quite excited; I mean she must know because she can read my aura.

I look at her with interest. "Do you think so Wanda? I mean I could certainly use some good news at this moment in time." Wanda laughs and Simone looks at me and grins.

"You know what Wanda I keep on telling her that she will be fine. I mean the world is full of hot guys and if she just opens her mind then she will have the time of her life." I roll my eyes. I know that it's not my mind Simone is intent on me opening and I throw her a warning look.

Wanda looks at us both and smiles. "Why don't you both come and join my class tomorrow at 11am. They are held upstairs and I think you could both use the escapism."

Simone looks interested. "What is it about?"

Wanda thrusts a leaflet at us. "Tantric yoga. It helps increase awareness between two people, enabling them to be in tune with each other's feelings and desires. Maybe when Winona here meets someone she will be schooled in the art of connection and it may help her weed out a few duds before she makes any mistakes. I mean I have seen it all before, fresh on the market women just settle for anyone they can get because they feel rejected by their husbands. It starts a cycle of negativity that pulls the poor woman down even further. I would hate that for you Winona, you need protecting from yourself if you don't mind me saying so and I think that I can help you."

Simone looks excited. "My God that sounds fantastic. I'm definitely in; I want to connect with my inner goddess too. I must say Wanda you have totally opened my eyes today I'm so glad we came here."

I nod enthusiastically and wonder if it's wrong of me to be just a little bit in love with my husband's new lover.

We can't stop talking about our amazing experience at Wanda's all the way home.

Simone looks at me thoughtfully. "You know even though this is all completely strange and totally against what I thought would happen today I am glad we went because now we have an invitation to investigate this woman further. I mean we have only been in her company for less than an hour and she has already recruited us into her cult. Maybe this is what happened to Lysander. He went there because of stress and she drugged him with her cake. Whilst his defences were down she convinced him that she was his soul mate and because he is now addicted to her drugs he will do anything she says. When you think about it it all makes sense."

I nod in agreement. "I think you're right, there I was wanting to hate every last thing about her but I have come away very much counting down the hours until tomorrow when we see her again. Funny how things work out."

We contemplate the situation silently for a moment and then I have a horrible thought. "Do you think that Lysander will be there, I don't think that I could bear it if he was?"

Simone shakes her head. "No he will probably be at work. He must attend the evening classes or he could have a private session with her after hours."

Weirdly we both burst out laughing at the thought of them practicing the tantric yoga after hours, I mean really it's not an image that I should have in my mind.

Simone says softly, "What are you going to do now Sophie? I mean we have arrived at a strange point in all this. You are now almost friends with the woman that has stolen your husband and will be spending rather a lot of time going forward with a certain sex god that there should be a government health warning about. One thing you must make sure though is that you never introduce Mr Rainford to Wanda. It appears that nobody is safe from that woman even us."

Chapter Thirteen

Luckily Simone picks Harry up from school to allow me to escape the question and answer session that will be definitely on the horizon from the mafia. I take the time to go for a long walk with Mr Tumnus instead to think about my new situation.

We set off through the woods and I am grateful for some alone time to really think about my situation. In just one week I have lost a husband to a weird drug dealing, tantric yoga teaching mother figure who I strangely want to be my friend. I have punched my husband and been comforted by the sexiest man alive who has offered me a job which involves spending most of my days with him. I have fallen into servitude and become the latest scandal. A lot can happen in a week that is for sure.

As Mr Tumnus runs around I head back the way I came. Luckily I don't see anyone and the fresh air does me a power of good. Out here in the countryside I can almost escape from what a nightmare my life is at the moment.

As we walk back along the pavement I spy a bucket of apples that somebody has left outside their gate for passers by to help themselves. Feeling in a creative perfect housewife mood all of a sudden I decide to grab some and intend on making something nice for pudding.

Using my fleece I parcel some up and feel quite

smug that I have foraged some free food. This may have to be my new hobby because one thing is for sure money is about to become extremely scarce.

As soon as we get home I set about my task. I decide to make some apple cake. Maybe it's because I can't get the memory out of my head of that delicious drug cake. I must get the recipe from Wanda when I see her tomorrow.

Soon the appetising smell of warm apples and cake wafts through the house and I decide to do a little bit of cleaning as I embrace my sudden domesticated self. Soon the whole house is cleaned from top to bottom and the sides are scrubbed and the clutter put away. I look around me with satisfaction. This is it, the new me. Perfect housewife perfection, Anthea could run her white gloves anywhere around here and there would be no dust to find.

The doorbell suddenly rings and I realise that it must be Simone bringing Harry home. He stayed at hers after school to play with Edward and she was going to give him his tea.

Dusting off my apron I fling the door open and then stare at the extremely unusual sight of Daniel filling up my doorway with his heavenly body.

As I look at him in total surprise he fixes me with his sexy eyes and grins causing my heart to do a triple axel and back flip. "I'm sorry to drop by Sophie but Harry forgot his Transformers and I know how attached these children get to their favourite toys. I was on my way home and thought that I would drop them in and discuss the job with you."

I look up at the sky and praise the almighty because despite this being my darkest hour it also strangely feels like my brightest.

I smile back suddenly conscious that I must smell of polish and dust and look like a complete mess.

"Thanks Daniel, you really shouldn't have gone to so much trouble it could have waited until tomorrow. But do come in and let me return the tea and biscuits favour."

As he follows me in I take several deep breaths. Thank god I cleaned the house and made the cake, images of Annabelle's dust palace spring to mind and I would hate him to think that I live like a pig as she does.

Feeling strangely flustered I lead him into the kitchen and switch on the kettle. I busy myself with the mugs and start to talk really fast which I always do when I'm nervous. "You know Daniel thank you for being so kind and supportive. I'm sure that it goes way past your job description and I just wanted to say that it has meant a lot to me. I mean life has been very strange this week and to be truthful I never saw any of it coming and what with having to carry on as usual and trying to throw the mafia off the scent it's all been a bit surreal really."

As I stop for breath I sneak a look at him and almost drop my panties right here and now. He is leaning back against the door of the kitchen looking at me with an extremely intense look. His eyes glitter and his mouth is twitching in amusement. I take in the sight of his lean body encased in the tightest of trousers and his shirt open at the neck showing the hint of a tanned muscular body beneath. There is a hint of stubble on his face and he exudes masculinity which in my extremely fragile state is like offering a drowning man a lifebelt.

He smiles sexily. "You don't have to thank me Sophie; I could tell that you needed a friend. I wasn't aware that you were being pursued by the mafia though."

I blush as I realise what I was rambling on about and he laughs. "Don't worry I know what you were referring to. Those other mums thrive on gossip and the more misery involved the better. I am sure that we are now the talk of the village."

I look at him and manage to squeak, "What do you mean....we?"

He smiles lazily. "Those women have seen us disappear into the classroom two days in a row. If they knew I was now in your kitchen then it would keep them going all year despite how innocent it is. I hope that I haven't added to your problems."

I smile softly. "I suppose I quite like being the subject of that sort of gossip. It might detract them from the knowledge that Lysander has ditched me in favour of a grandmother."

Daniel looks at me in shock and I laugh sadly. "It's true. Simone and I went to see her today; we knew that she had a shop in town. I wasn't prepared to find someone in there who could be his mother and to tell you the truth I really liked her. In fact I am booked in to her....um yoga class tomorrow to discover my inner goddess."

Daniel looks at me and then laughs loudly. I join in and that is exactly the sight that greets Simone as she pushes Harry through the back door into the room. There is silence as we all stare at each other. Harry slides his hand in mine and looks worried. Daniel smiles at him. "Don't worry Harry I've only come to bring your Transformers. You left them at school and I know how attached you are to them."

Harry looks at him in relief. I nudge him and he lisps, "Thank you Mr Rainford."

I smile at him gratefully. Simone looks between us and fixes me with a look that says I told you so. Daniel straightens up and smiles. "Listen I won't keep you but remember to drop by tomorrow either before or after school to see Mrs Fletcher. She will fill you in on everything and maybe you could start next week whilst she shows you the ropes."

I nod and then with a pointed look towards Simone I show Daniel out.

Chapter Fourteen

Simone won't leave until I tell her every last detail and when I finish she smirks at me. "See I told you he had the hots for you, Transformers my arse." I roll my eyes. "Careful Simone Harry could hear you and you know how impressionable he is at the moment. If I hear him use the "a" word then I'm holding you completely responsible."

Simone takes another piece of the apple cake that we are systematically demolishing between us. "We had better finish this off tonight and then we can work it off in the yoga session tomorrow."

I nod in agreement. "I can't wait can you? I mean Wanda certainly knows her stuff. Take a look around you. Less than one hour in her company and I have re-grouped and organised my home. I have made bakery products from foraged food and enjoyed a pleasant conversation with the equivalent to David Beckham in my newly disinfected kitchen.

Tomorrow I am connecting with my inner goddess and polishing my aura. Quite a productive day really."

Simone grins. "Good for you. Now I must get home because Martin is waiting to eat. Sweet dreams my foot loose and fancy free friend and just make sure you dream about that hot teacher rather than pining away for lying Lysander."

The next day comes and I set off with trepidation towards the playground. I have timed it earlier than normal so that I may escape the mafia and connect with Mrs Fletcher. Harry chatters incessantly as we make our way there and once again I feel guilty that the theme tune to Postman Pat has been replaced in my mind with Ellie Goulding's Fifty Shades theme tune. "Love me like you do."

Luckily we manage to make it into school unobserved and whilst Harry learns his spellings Mrs Fletcher takes me through what I need to know. I fill in all of her relevant forms and promise to report for duty at 8.45am on Monday morning.

Just before the bell rings for the start of the day my heart flips as Daniel comes into the office and invades it with his heavenly scent. I notice that even Mrs Fletcher straightens up and flicks her hair before fixing him with a rare smile from the usually austere admin assistant.

Daniel smiles sexily at me and winks almost making me faint on the spot. I feel a hot flush coming on and wonder if it is the menopause coming early brought on by the shocks of the last week.

Daniel grins. "Good to see you Mrs Bailey. I hope that you will enjoy working here just as much I will enjoy having you."

He smiles a secret smile as he heads off to collect his charges and leaves me with a very uncomfortable feeling between my legs.

Mrs Fletcher smiles at me.

"You know I almost put off my retirement because of him. Working here has been a lot more interesting since he came here. It's no hardship working with a man that looks like a movie star."

I smile and feel myself blushing as I try to look uninterested. "Yes I suppose so, not that I've really noticed, I mean all of that is behind me, or at least I thought it was."

Mrs Fletcher looks at me with concern. "I know I heard the news. I'm so sorry Mrs Bailey. It's awful and I hope that it all resolves itself quickly and amicably for all your sakes."

I look at her and frown. "Me too Mrs Fletcher. The last thing I want is for it to get ugly."

Chapter Fifteen

"NOW IT GETS UGLY" I scream at Simone as I wave the letter that I received just before she picked me up for Tantric Yoga. She looks at me with concern and says gently, "Calm down Sophie, what's happened?"

I sit down heavily and thrust the letter towards her. Lysander has sent me a solicitor's letter that states that he is divorcing me on the grounds of irreconcilable differences. What on earth is he playing at? I should be divorcing him on the grounds of his adultery. What are the differences he talks about? Wanting to watch a different channel to him, or choosing to drink coffee instead of tea, I mean it's a joke."

Simone looks at me with a hard expression. "Don't worry Soph I spoke to my sister last night and she told me that Mimi wants to arrange an appointment with you. I am to ask if you're free tomorrow afternoon."

I stare at her with grim determination. "You bet your ass I am. What time?" Simone grins. "3pm, I'll have Harry after school whilst you sort that bastard out."

Feeling slightly calmer I look at her with a worried expression. "Does she know that I don't have any money?"

Simone smiles. "It's a favour to my sister, I told you. You get your divorce settlement and she gets her preferred school. Apparently my sister had to bump someone off the list to include her daughter Imogen. It certainly pays to have friends in high places."

I look at Simone gratefully. "Thanks hon, I haven't actually said this but thank you. Not just for the solicitor but for being such an amazing friend. I don't think I could do this without you."
Simone smiles sadly. "I wish you didn't have to. I know that this is hurting you and despite my flippant nature I know that you are devastated. I'm always here for you remember that, you're not on your own. Although I may replace you with Wanda as my bestie if she keeps on feeding me that cake." I grin. "Right back at you."

As we arrive we notice that there are many other women milling around in the corridor above her shop. I look with interest at my fellow Tantric lovers and note that most appear to be normal. There are only about two men and about 10 women. All look like they mean business and sport many a designer fitness label. I on the other hand quickly headed to Primark to buy the cheapest outfit I could. Knowing me my new found passion will only last the week before I get bored and move on to decoupage or some other craft related hobby.
Wanda appears resplendent in a purple shell suit with lime green stripes down the side. Her hair is tamed into some sort of braided style and she ushers us all

in to her studio.

There are several yoga mats on the floor and a cracked mirror adorns the length of the wall.

Everyone takes their positions, as whale music once again invades the room.

By the time we have finished I feel in tune with every last person here. I know what they are doing and sense their every move. I am a bit worried that I may have developed feelings for Simone and resolve never to come here again. Wanda it would seem can manipulate anyone to do her bidding and I feel completely out of my depth.

Simone and I are fairly subdued on the way home. As we drive in she looks at me. "I don't think we should go there again do you?"

I nod and she says, "I don't know why but I started picturing every one around me in sexual positions and if she had told us to have an orgy I probably would have joined in."

I grin at her. "Yes I know what you mean. Maybe we had better stick to Pilates in the village hall. We've still got the cake though. Do you want to come in for some?"

Simone grins. "As long as you're talking about the cake then yes you try and stop me." We head inside laughing.

I decide to pick Harry up from school and take him to see the latest kid's film at the cinema. I know that I should be watching the pennies but I feel disconnected from him and want to indulge him whilst I can. We are going to have our tea out and he was super excited about it this morning when I mentioned it.

As I walk into the playground I feel the stares. Groups of women huddle together and throw pointed looks in my direction. I don't even have Simone for moral support because she picked Edward up early for a doctor's appointment.

One of Harry's friends mum catches my eye and smiles at me encouragingly. She looks around her and then heads over to me. "Hi Sophie, how are you?" She fixes me with a sympathetic look and the way she said it was extremely insincere.

I smile and put on my brave face. "Oh I'm fine thank you Claire. Despite what has happened I am just moving on with things and not letting it get me down."

She gives me that look that says that she knows that I am just putting on a brave face and as she looks around her she lowers her voice. "Listen you're not alone in this situation. Karen Mulligan's husband left her last month but he came back when he realised that it would cost him too much to divorce her and Sadie Carmichael had an affair with her fitness instructor and when her husband found out they had a fight and the police were called. You know despite what image everyone portrays in this playground it is a very different picture behind closed doors. Take Annabelle Buckley for instance. I know that her husband has an affair a month and they are into all sorts within their group in that Country club."

Now she has my full attention and despite myself I lean in for more information. "Really Claire, I never knew, how do you know this stuff?"

Claire smiles in a strangely sinister way. "I keep my ear to the ground and my eyes open. Don't you worry your husband's affair with an older woman and your fixation on Mr Rainford is small fry compared with what else goes on."

She is called away and leaves me in total shock. MY FIXATION WITH MR RAINFORD!!!!

Ok actually she does have a point, maybe I do have a small crush on him but I'm not alone there, add in every other mother here and there is quite a queue to join. I don't get to think about it all too much before the doors open and normal service is resumed.

After my daily fix of Daniel I whisk Harry off to the cinema and just lose myself in the world of a six year old.

Chapter Sixteen

Harry and I have a great time at the cinema. I never knew that having a child would be so much fun. Finally I get to spend hours of time just watching animated movies whilst eating popcorn without feeling guilty about it.

Harry actually wasn't that interested in watching Frozen but I sort of talked him into it, I mean the latest Disney Pixar movie can wait until it's out on DVD. Frozen on the other hand waits for no one. We wrap up the evening with a MacDonald's happy meal each and by the time we get home its time for bath and story time.

As I read him his favourite book, Harry Potter and The Chamber of Secrets, I feel as if my heart is being ripped from inside me whilst still beating. Feeling his sleepy warm body cuddling into mine I hate Lysander more than I ever thought I would. How can he throw all of this...us away for a middle aged fling? I know that this is exactly what it is. We were happy, we never argued and I wasn't a demanding wife. Harry is a good boy and we had everything. Why didn't he tell me if he wasn't feeling happy? I just don't get it. They say that women are more intuitive than men but in this case he has wiped the emotional floor with me.

Harry's breathing steadies and I kiss his soft head loathe to release him. Instead I just settle back against the pillows and close my eyes, trying to stop the tears from escaping. It's just me, Harry and Mr Tumnus now, who is snoring on the other side of me, snuggled in for the night. This is it, my new world and I will work as hard as is humanly possible to make them proud. They are everything to me now and nothing will ever stop me from putting them first.

It must be about 2am that I wake up and realise that I fell asleep. Harry has slid down and is curled up in a tight ball under his Transformers duvet cover. Mr Tumnus has moved to the end of the bed where I can hear his growly snores disturbing the otherwise deathly silence. Carefully I ease out of the bed and after making sure that Harry is tucked in head back to my room.

Once I am ready I climb into bed on *my side* as usual and try to get back to sleep. The trouble is now I am awake everything starts to rush around in my mind. I can't believe that I am now in this position. The house feels different now, sort of empty and lifeless. One very important person is missing and there is nothing I can do about it. I feel rejected and abandoned and I absolutely hate the part of me that still wishes that he would come back.

Maybe he will wake up tomorrow and realise that it was all a mistake. Maybe he will come rushing back and beg for my forgiveness and say that he will spend the rest of his life making it up to me. Maybe he will but probably he won't.

As I turn over my hand reaches over to the now cold side of the bed. It feels empty and abandoned just like I do and at this moment in time in the middle of the night I feel more alone than I have ever felt in my life before.

I am not sure how much sleep I got but the sound of Mr Tumnus barking wakes me up. Looking over at the alarm clock I jump up in a panic as I realise that I must have forgotten to set it. It is 9am and we are now extremely late for school.

Suddenly I am Robo Mum and I move around Cornish Cottage like a tornado. In approximately 30 minutes Harry is up, dressed and ready for school and I have barely had time to throw a coat over my pyjamas and my wellies on before we are running down the road towards the school humming the theme tune to Thunderbirds.

The playground is deserted-thank goodness and I ring the bell at the main office for somebody to let us in. Whilst we wait I silently pray that it will be Mrs Fletcher, given the state of me. The just got out of bed look is not a good one, especially when you may be faced with the perfection that is housed within these walls.

No such luck though as the door flings open revealing the mouth watering sight of Mr Rainford. I try to look nonchalant as he slowly looks me up and down and a smile breaks out across his face and his eyes glitter with amusement. "Mrs Bailey and Harry, good morning to you both. Running a bit late I see." I look down and mumble, "Um sorry I'm afraid the alarm clock failed and we slept in. I hope that it hasn't inconvenienced you too much?" Mr Rainford smiles. "These things happen its no big deal." He turns to Harry and says, "Run off to class Harry, I'll be along in a minute, you know where to hang your coat." Harry does as he is told and feeling very uncomfortable I turn away saying over my shoulder, "I'll leave you to it then."

Suddenly I feel a hand on my arm and I almost jump out of my rather shabby coat as Mr Rainford grips my arm tightly and spins me around to face him. He looks down and smiles gently.

"Rough night?" His kindness totally undoes me and I bite my lip to stem the every present tears. He has seen more than enough of my crying face to last me a lifetime. I shake myself and try to muster a bright smile.

"No really we're fine. We just overslept that's all. It's my fault I shouldn't have taken him to the cinema on a school night. I'm sorry it won't happen again."

Mr Rainford keeps his hand on my arm and in my mind I picture him pulling me towards him and declaring his undying love for me before kissing me passionately before taking me in the stationery cupboard in every way possible.

Instead he just smiles softly and releases my arm.

"You know I'm here any time you need someone to

talk to Sophie. Remember we're friends now not to mention soon to be work colleagues. You can always count on me to sound off to you know."

I smile gratefully. "Thank you, that means a lot to me Mr Rai...I mean Daniel."

I look into his gentle brown eyes and swallow hard before shaking myself and laughing nervously say, "Well I should get home. I need to get ready and walk the dog. Oh and I nearly forgot Simone will be collecting Harry after school because I have an appointment with my solicitor."

Daniel looks surprised. "Are you going on your own?"

I nod sadly. "Yes, unless they allow dogs I am afraid that I and myself are all I have at the moment. I'm sure I'll be fine though, I mean how bad can it possibly be?"

With one last smile I turn away and leave him standing there. What I wouldn't give for someone to look after me for once.

Chapter Seventeen

I am sitting waiting nervously in an extremely impressive reception area. "Simmonds, Simmonds and Simmonds" is emblazoned on the wall behind the receptionist and I fleetingly wonder why one Simmonds isn't enough. What happens if someone joins who isn't called Simmonds? It could be that only Simmonds need apply or a name change by deed poll is a pre-requisite for the job.

I look around and study the corporate interior. It is extremely stark and is full of chrome and steel with splashes of red and black lasered through with silver on their logo. There is a water cooler in the corner and a few strategically placed magazines on a low slung table.

After having briskly flicked through them I quickly realise that they are not the usual Ok and Hello that I have come to expect, but then this is hardly the hairdressers.

The last thing I want to read about is Architectural monthly and self help leaflets so instead I pull out my phone and type in a tweet.

About to face the lion's den. Wish me luck as I may not make it out alive.

I wait a few seconds and then look for any notifications. Hmm none, that's annoying. I would have at least expected a retweet or a like by now. In fact someone has just unfollowed me. Now I feel even more desperate. Even my Twitter friends are leaving me. In fact my virtual friends are really not shaping up lately; I may even have to pay for followers to make myself feel loved again.

As I frown at my phone I hear a loud noise coming from one of the offices as the door opens and a smart looking man comes out. Before the door shuts I hear an angry voice shouting, "Nobody gets the better of me, you're going down you son of a bitch and you will never recover. Take that you slime ball and take what's coming to you." The door closes and I look at the young rather attractive man in shock.

Catching my eye he smiles and rolls his eyes. "She won't keep you long. Sorry for the delay."

I just nod and try to smile but I am sure that it looks more like a grimace. Goodness I had heard she was a tough cookie but that was something else. I almost pity Lysander at this moment in time.

It must be 5minutes later that the receptionist takes a call and then looks at me and smiles almost pityingly. "Ms Constable will see you now, go on through."

I jump up in alarm and smooth down my dress. I have taken Simone's advice and power dressed for the occasion. I am wearing a black smart dress with a little matching jacket and smart black stilettos. She told me that I must look like I mean business and so it is this thought that I try to hold on to as I head off into the lion's den.

As I open the door I see a huge window dominating the wall in front of me. In front of it is a desk at which sits the formidable Ms Constable.

She looks at me with a hard stare and I feel as if I have entered the headmistresses study. I can feel her staring at me taking in every inch of my appearance and to say I feel uncomfortable is an understatement. Suddenly she smiles and stands up offering me her hand and gestures to the seat in front of her desk.

"You must be Sophie, Alison's friend. I'm Mimi, pleased to meet you."

Feeling somewhat taken off guard I just smile politely and shake her hand as I sit down opposite her.

Mimi looks at me and frowns. "I've heard your sorry tale and I actually can't wait to get started. Men are such bastards and think they can run rings around us women."

She leans forward and grins wickedly. "I have made it my mission statement to bring every last cheating one of them down and leave them with nothing but their traitorous dicks for company."

She leans back and smiles with satisfaction leaving me with a very disturbing image of Lysander living with his Dick as she put it in poverty. Actually the way I am feeling at the moment the image does bring a certain smile to my face.

Seeing it she grins and punches a button on a

machine next to her. "Kim, bring us in two coffees will you and some of those jammy dodgers that you keep for the visitor's children. We need some energy in this room to get us fit for battle."

She smiles and then laughs a slightly evil maniacal laugh that leaves me feeling strangely worried for my safety.

"Right then, first things first don't worry about the bill for all of this because it has been taken care of. When we bleed that sucker dry it will be all yours. Call this a pro bono case, I don't usually do these but I have certain needs myself and this is worth every penny to get my beloved Imogen into the best school in town. So that said we can crack on without any worries, agreed."

I nod and just manage to stutter out, "You are very kind to do this." She waves her hand. "No I'm not; kind is the last thing I am as you will soon find out. No your lying, cheating, wife and child abandoning husband is just about to find out how unkind I can be."

We are interrupted as Kim brings in the coffee and biscuits. I am slightly intrigued to see that Mimi puts a whole one in her mouth almost immediately and almost swallows it whole. Thrusting the plate that is piled high with virtually the whole packet towards me she barks, "Help yourself, you're going to need the energy."

For some reason Annabelle and her carb free friends spring to my mind as I bite into the deliciously forbidden sugar infested biscuit that spells danger on every level.

Leaning back Mimi takes a swig of her coffee and then reaches for a brown manila envelope on the table beside her. She opens it and spreads out some photographs and I can see with surprise that they are of Lysander.

Looking at me with a hard expression she says, "I had my investigator friend rustle these up for me so that I could see what we're dealing with. I believe that these pictures are of your husband and his fancy piece. Take a look will you and confirm it."

Shaking I reach over not really sure that I want to see the evidence in front of me. I mean its one thing to see Wanda in person on her own but to see them together will be extremely hard.

I pull them towards me and will myself to look at them. However it is not Wanda that I see with him but a tall, slim much younger woman with long black hair wearing jeans and a vest top. They are holding hands and she is gazing up at him adoringly. I feel sick as I see the closeness between them and then I get an even greater shock as I look at my husband. He is wearing jeans-he never wears jeans-and a cheesecloth shirt open at the neck with a man necklace around his throat. On his wrists are those friendship bands and he is wearing flip flops. He is looking at her with adoration and despite the shock I just think how ridiculous he looks.

I look up at Mimi with wide eyes and she grins.

"Shocked are you? Well I'm not. This is the typical attire of a man trying to recapture his youth. Look at them. She is obviously much younger than he is and probably can't believe her luck that she has a sugar daddy lavishing everything he can on to her. Gold digging Trollope if ever I saw one. These young girls don't care about his family, they have no morals and only care about what's in it for them. Mark my words he will be dropped from a great height when the money dries up and she will be on to the next poor unsuspecting fool. He will then realise his mistake and come crawling back. You in the meantime will have been empowered and will see him in a new light. You will have moved on mentally and physically and will also have no further use for him. Well until that day darling we are going to have so much fun bringing him down."

I smile weakly at her and can't really see any of that happening. To tell you the truth I feel in total shock and I realise sadly that shock is becoming quite a habit. Seeing Lysander with this young girl is actually worse than Wanda. Suddenly I am being replaced by a younger, fitter model who looks like she is making him very happy indeed.

I can feel Mimi watching me carefully and I try to pull myself together. She leans forward and fixes me with an intense look.

"Do you play the Xbox Sophie?" I look at her in surprise and shake my head. "No I don't. Harry has one but I wouldn't know the first thing about it."

Mimi grins. "I wouldn't be without mine. It's such a great stress reliever. I play it all the time. In fact I was on it before you came in. Any time that I feel the need to vent I don my battle sim and pulverise my virtual opponent. I can highly recommend it. What you need now if you don't mind me saying is to either embrace the battleground of your son's Xbox or go and get laid. Either one will make you feel a whole lot better; it's your choice."

I look at her in shock. Goodness, Xbox or sex. Both fill me with utter terror. I mean it's been years since I had sex with anyone other than Lysander and even then there wasn't much of a line before him. The thought of being intimate with anyone else strikes me with absolute terror.

The trouble is so does the Xbox. I've only just mastered the art of the i phone, Harry is much better at technology than me and he is only six years old. If this is my future then I am seriously screwed.

Mimi pushes one of the photographs towards me. "Here take this Sophie. Every time you feel that you're weakening look at this image. It will give you the strength for the fight and you will need a lot of that. Meanwhile I will be writing to your husband's solicitor and petitioning him for divorce on the grounds of his adultery. What do you want me to say regarding your son and visiting rights for the time being?"

I shake myself and look at her with a terrified expression. "I don't know really. I mean I don't want

Harry to be affected by all of this as much as possible and so if Lysander wants to see him then it is fine with me."

Mimi nods. "Ok leave it with me. I will copy you in on the letter and email you the details. Fill out this form and hand it in to Kim and we will start the laborious process."

She looks at me thoughtfully. "You know this could take years. I just want to warn you. Hopefully we can come to a mutual quick settlement without the need for a court hearing. I am sure that we can get this wrapped up quickly if we are all on the same page."

She stands up and offers me her hand. As I shake it I almost wince with the pain. She has a crushing hand shake, a bit like the woman herself really.

She nods and smiles. "Remember Sophie, get out there soon and get yourself some self esteem back. You are an attractive woman and won't be on your own for long if that is what you want. Don't leave it too long otherwise it will get harder. If that fails embrace the Xbox instead, I can't recommend it highly enough."

I smile and thank her and then head outside clutching the photograph and the form, both of them well and truly signifying the end of my marriage.

Chapter Eighteen

I start the journey home and think about everything that has just happened. I still can't get my head around the fact that I have been traded in for a younger model. Model is the word as this new girlfriend could definitely be one.

I can feel the tears burning behind my eyes and at this moment in time I feel as low as I have ever felt in my life. I feel old, used and cast aside. I will need to learn the Xbox and fast because nobody would want to have sex with a washed up old reject like me anyway.

As I sit on the bus home I contemplate my life. Now it's as real as it gets and it will be down to me to navigate the future. It is almost certain that I will have to move, probably to a shared flat somewhere. I will probably have to claim benefits because I don't earn any money. I may even have to get the number for the local food bank because once the apples and blackberries have dried up there will be no more free foraged food.

I bite my lip and look around me. It appears that the whole world has found love as happy couples are everywhere. Mothers are pushing prams looking safe and secure unlike me. I am now well and truly on my own. All I have is Harry, Simone and Mr Tumnus and my Facebook and Twitter friends. Surely this is my darkest hour. Things can only get better - can't they?

By the time I reach Simone's house to pick Harry up I am feeling as low as can be. This is it, I am officially beaten. There is no hope for me, all I have to look forward to is watching Harry grow up and become the man I know he can be. He would never do to his wife what his father has done to me. I will raise him to respect women and to be open about his feelings. From now on he will be my mission statement and nobody better get in my way because I will be like a human battle sim where he is concerned and pulverise anyone who hurts or upsets him.

Simone takes one look at my face as she opens the door and pulls me inside shouting, "Martin, keep the boys happy I'm just having a drink with Sophie in the kitchen."
I hear him shout, "Ok babes, hi Soph good to almost see you." Despite myself I smile. I like Martin. He is easy going which he most definitely has to be living with Simone. I shout back although it does sound a little strained. "Hi Martin, thanks for everything."
Before he can reply Simone pulls me into the kitchen and reaches for the wine.
I am soon nursing a huge glass of Cabernet and telling Simone the whole sorry tale.
As I finish she looks at me in shock and then the tears fill her eyes and she reaches over and grasps my hand. "I'm so sorry Soph, what a pig."

I nod in wholehearted agreement. "So what's next then? Will it be the Xbox or the sex box?" I stifle a small smile.

"It will have to be the Xbox although both fill me with complete horror. To tell you the truth I just want to go home and curl up in a tight miserable ball and cry myself to sleep. I can honestly say I feel emotionally wrung out and thinking about what comes next is terrifying me."

Simone looks at me with sympathy. "You'll get through it you're stronger than you think." I nod miserably. "Anyway I'd better round up my cowboy and head for the hills. It's been a long day and I am just glad that it's Friday and I don't have any plans this weekend. Maybe it will give me some much needed thinking time." Simone nods and then shouts for the boys.

By the time we get home it is full on bed time routine and by the time I have got Harry safely bathed and read him a story all thoughts that I have about my situation are firmly parked to the back of my mind.

I settle down in front of the TV to distract myself when the phone rings. My heart sinks when I hear Lysander's voice and I tense up steeling myself for the conversation to come.

"Hi Sophie, sorry to ring last minute and all but I was wondering if I could have Harry this weekend. I haven't seen him and I've missed him not to mention the fact that he will be missing me too." Taking a deep breath I try to keep my voice from shaking with the hurt and the anger that I am feeling towards him. Harry has to come first and despite the fact that I hate the very thought I know that Lysander is right.

"What did you have in mind?"

He says brightly. "Well I could pick him up in the morning and take him for the weekend. I will show him my new house and his new room and generally spoil him. We may take in a film or go to that new Adventure Barn that's opened in Aldershot near the Army barracks, he would love that, and so would I actually."

He laughs and my stomach churns at the light way he is speaking. I grit my teeth. "Will she be there?" I have to know because I can't bear the thought of some other woman playing happy families with my husband and son when it should be me.

He says softly. "No, Ocean is visiting friends this weekend. I could have gone but I wanted to see Harry."

I snort. "How very good of you. Let me put your name forward for father of the year."

There is a long silence and then he says in a low voice. "There's no need for that. Let's just keep this amicable for all our sakes. The fact that I am passing up the chance for a weekend away with Ocean to have Harry must cancel out any bad feelings that you have towards me. I'm only trying to do the best for everyone you know."

Swallowing the acid retort that instantly springs to

my lips I merely say angrily, "Ok then 10am sharp. He will be ready with his overnight bag. Don't be late." Then I hang up the phone and burst into tears of rage. Who the hell calls their daughter OCEAN?!!!!

The next morning Harry is super excited to be seeing his father and chatters incessantly. I try to look normal but my heart is tearing in two at the thought of him leaving me for the weekend.

This is obviously what my future holds. Fractured family sharing their son's life. Part time mother and father both with their own agendas. The fact that Lysander appears to have already created his happy ever after is just the icing on the cake.

The doorbell rings and I steel myself to see my errant husband since I punched him in the face.

Harry screams at him and throws himself at his father and a lump forms in my throat as I see how excited he is. Despite what has happened Lysander is a good father and I see the genuine love and relief in his face as he cuddles his son.

I look away loathe to feel anything but hatred for the man in front of me.

Lysander straightens up and takes Harry's bag from me and smiles softly.

"I'll bring him home at 7pm on Sunday. Take the chance to have a rest Sophie, you look like you could do with it, I mean I don't think I've ever seen you look so tired." He turns to Harry. "Hug your mother Harry and then we'll roll."

Harry grabs hold of me and his little arms squeeze me tightly. I blink back the tears and just kiss him on the top of his head. "Be good little man. I love you to the moon and back- remember?" He smiles happily. "I love you too mummy."
And then they go, my once perfect family walking away from me down the path leaving me all alone.

Chapter Nineteen

With a heavy heart I decide to take Mr Tumnus for a long walk to try and clear my head. I grab his lead and a bag for any free food that we may come across and head outside.

It's actually a nice sunny autumn morning and the leaves are beginning to turn rendering everything spectacular around me.

The sun warms my spirit and I laugh at Mr Tumnus as he runs free and without a care in the world. The sad fact is that I now wish I was my dog because his life is so much better than mine.

We must have been out for a least two hours and I am feeling quite proud of myself for harvesting some apples, plums and blackberries from within the hedgerows or from the plastic boxes laid out on the grass verges in front of people's gardens with signs telling you to *help yourself.*

I have decided to spend the afternoon making apple sauce and jam. Just what the doctor ordered, comfort food to mend a broken heart.

I am suddenly aware of the unmistakeable sight of Annabelle Buckley's Range Rover slowing down beside me. She winds down the window and shouts, "Wait up Sophie."

Sighing inwardly I stop and fix her with a bright smile, the total opposite to what I am feeling inside.

She fixes me with her rather false smile and looks at me sympathetically.

"I'm sorry to hear your terrible news Sophie. How are you bearing up?"

I maintain a dignified pose and just shrug. "Thank you Annabelle, I'm fine as it happens." Gosh liar of the year award goes to Sophie Bailey!

She smiles which I notice doesn't quite reach her eyes.

"Listen Sophie I hope that you don't mind me saying but usually in these situations money gets a bit tight and I might just be able to help you there."

I look at her in surprise.

"What do you mean Annabelle?" She grins.

"Well I am looking for someone to help out with the household chores. Just a few hours a week, you know housework and stuff, maybe a spot of babysitting here and there and I thought that I would give you first refusal." She waves her hand and laughs shrilly. "Now don't you go thanking me, its not charity I was going to hire someone anyway but when I heard about your sorry situation I wanted to help. I mean what are friends for? I will pay you in cash; shall we say £15 an hour? I know it's more than the minimum rate, I mean I would hate to offer that to anybody."

I can't believe what I am hearing and am actually speechless. She looks at me with a hard expression.

"Well what do you say? I mean you could work it around Harry and if I know how these things work you may have your weekends free. That way you will be earning money and it will give you something to do."

Well I can't argue with her there so I just smile weakly.

"You're very kind Annabelle. Obviously I'd love to help you. When do you need me to start?"

She looks at me and smiles almost with relief which strikes me as odd.

"How about today say immediately. I can show you the ropes and then you can get stuck in. Shall we say about three hours?"

I nod and then wave towards Mr Tumnus.

"I'll just take him home and meet you at yours if you like."

Throwing the car door open she says briskly, "That's fine, jump in and bring the dog. He can play with Bessie in the garden. They can wear each other out."

I climb in feeling completely surprised. I almost feel as if I am being kidnapped and will be imprisoned in her dust palace as a slave.

Luckily her house isn't far so I don't have to make polite conversation with her for too long before we pull in to her drive.

I follow her into the house and once again take in the sight of the chaos that is her home.

She marches into the kitchen and once again thrusts the obligatory apron towards me.

"Right then, let's put the animals outside and then you can make a start in here. The cleaning bucket is under the sink and you should find everything you need in there. There's not much more to say other than the oven could use a good scrub too. Now I am afraid that I am going to have to love you and leave you because I have a class at the country club. Sebastian is somewhere upstairs doing god only knows what and Daisy is watching a DVD in the living room. I should only be three hours tops which should work out just fine."

Before I can answer she sweeps out of the room leaving me to close my mouth that has dropped open in disbelief. If I wasn't feeling quite so used I would be extremely impressed at such a carefully executed operation.

After letting the dogs out I set to work. Maybe cleaning will take my mind off things and I can challenge my rage into something more productive. Unfortunately Annabelle's cleaning things are sadly not up to the job and make everything even more difficult than they have to be.

I start on the oven and almost heave at the sight of the food encrusted racks and thick layer of grease on every surface. She doesn't even have rubber gloves and so now my hands will be shot to pieces.

It must be an hour into my scrubbing that the kitchen door opens and Daisy runs into the room.

I smile at her and she grins showing me the gaps in her teeth. "Hello Sophie can I have a biscuit and a cup of tea please?" I put down my grease soaked cloth and smile at her.

"Of course you can darling. Come and sit down and tell me all about the DVD you are watching whilst I make it for you."

She drags the heavy chair out and sits at the table talking non stop about the film. I am actually enjoying hearing her little high pitched voice ringing out and with a pang realise that I had always wanted a sister for Harry. We could do girly things like bake cookies and paint necklaces.

I make her the drink and say, "Do you think your brother would like one too?" She frowns and looks thoughtful. "He would probably prefer a beer." I look at her in surprise. "What in the middle of the day?" She shrugs. "Why not?"

I turn away before she sees me grin. Why not indeed?

I make him a tea anyway and one for myself. After telling Daisy to go and fetch her brother I try to clear the table free from the various papers and books that litter it so that we can have our tea safely without the fear of spilling it all over the paperwork.

Daisy returns with a surly looking teenager who has long dark shoulder length hair and is wearing a beanie hat. He is also sporting the latest headphones and just nods at me as I smile at him.

"You must be Sebastian; I'm Sophie, pleased to meet you." He nods and then grabs the mug and a few biscuits and retreats from the room.

By the time we have finished the tea I have learned

rather a lot from young Daisy. She talks about her family a lot and I hear all the gossip from the playground. I now know that she hates Crystal Waters - yet another daft name - and has a crush on Jordan Cunningham. Her favourite teacher is Miss Barley the teaching assistant and her best friend is Megan Somerville.

Whilst I carry on with the oven she helps me by washing up the mugs and tidying around. I can see the dogs fighting on the lawn and find to my surprise that I am actually really enjoying myself.

Daisy gets bored after an hour and heads back to DVD land. I have finally finished the oven and set about trying to clean the kitchen.

It seems that in no time at all Annabelle is back.

"Sophie, you're a marvel. I knew that I could count on you. Same time next week?"

I smile and shrug. "If I don't have Harry then I would love to." Annabelle waves her hand.

"Well if you do then just bring him with you. He can play with Daisy or watch the TV. This could work well in both our favours."

She hands me some money and as I take in the sight of the notes in my hand I feel that she is right. This could definitely work in my favour.

Chapter Twenty

By the time I get home I feel a little bit more optimistic. I know that cleaning for lady muck - in the literal sense isn't one of my life's ambitions but it's a start. I also have my new job at the school to look forward to so in a way life is looking up a little. I decide to start making my jam when I get in and set about the task, pretending that I am Nigella as I get everything ready.

I start talking to myself and float around the kitchen like the domesticated goddess that I am, pretending that I am the food guru, striking sultry poses and flicking my hair towards an imaginary camera.

This actually isn't the first time I have done this. Nigella is my preferred sex kitten chef but I have been known to imitate Delia on the odd occasion.

The trouble is I am now more Gordon Ramsey as I swear at the jam that is burning on the bottom of the pan.

Luckily I am saved by the bell and grab the phone that is ringing nearby.

"Sophie Bailey, domesticated goddess and master chef, how may I help you?"

"Soph you twit it's me Simone. Where have you been?"

"Slaving away cleaning Annabelle flaming Buckley's public health warning of an oven."

"WHAT! Why on earth were you doing that?"

"Because she paid me mighty handsomely for it after kidnapping me off the street and forcing me once again into servitude."

Simone giggles. "I bet it was disgusting the dirty cow. I'm not surprised she's paying you to scrub her dust ridden flea pit of a kitchen though. Probably doesn't want to ruin her gel polish."

I laugh whilst juggling a jam thermometer and the phone just praying that I don't dunk the wrong one into the pan of boiling liquid.

"Listen Soph I know you're on your own tonight so do you fancy a night out? We could check out that new wine bar in town, you know the one with the fit guys on the door. I've been dying to go there since it opened and now I have the perfect excuse."

I roll my eyes. "Which is?"

"Comforting my friend in her hour of need. Martin is taking Edward to see his mother and you know that we can't stand each other so this was my get out of mother-in-law hell visit free card."

I grin into the phone.

"Well if you put it like that what time shall we meet?"

"I'll pick you up at 8pm. Dress to impress as they say because I fully intend on working on your distraction therapy as recommended by our very own bitch face solicitor friend."

Shaking my head I hang up the phone. Simone is as nutty as a fruit cake and I couldn't wish for a better friend than her. If I didn't have her I would be curled up with Mr Tumnus for company and become a recluse. I would be called the "*Dog*" lady who lives with her animals in a different world to the rest of society.

Finally I bottle up the blackberry jam into several of the jam jars that I have collected for various craft projects and set about cleaning up the mess.

After several changes of clothing and various attempts at styling my hair I am finally ready. I have tried to curl my hair with the tongs like Zoella showed me on You Tube. The little black dress that I am wearing was a bargain from Zara in the sale and the black stilettos were a charity shop find in one of the wealthier parts of town.

I must say it feels really strange to be going out on the town and I feel a little bit silly if I'm honest. Normally I would be curled up next to Lysander by now watching X Factor or Strictly. I can't even remember the last time I went out to a wine bar. What if they're all teenagers? We will stick out like sore thumbs.

Simone picks me up at 8pm on the dot and grins at me. She is wearing not a dissimilar outfit to mine and she grabs my hand and pulls me after her.

"Come on then, mission re-bound is well and truly underway."

I look at her guiltily. "Did Martin mind you coming out with me? I wouldn't have thought that Lysander would have liked it if the ball had been on the other foot."

Sophie shrugs. "I just told him we were going into town for a drink. He trusts me and knows that I wouldn't do anything. You are my number one priority at the moment and the last thing I want is for you to spend your first weekend on your own with just Mr Tumnus for company."

I smile at her gratefully. "You're a true friend, you know that Simone Fitzpatrick?" She grins.

"Yeah salt of the earth, a real diamond. The fact is Soph I actually can't wait to take this journey with you. You have so much to give the right man. Lysander is a fool for letting you go. You just need to believe in yourself and let yourself go. I'm betting that your future is bright Sophie Bailey and I am going to be beside you all the way."

I reach out and grab her hand squeezing it gently. "Thank you Simone. I don't deserve you."

She pushes me playfully. "Of course you do you soppy date. Come on let's go and have some fun."

Chapter Twenty One

The Blue Banana is the latest Bar to open in the nearby town and I'm not going to lie my stomach is churning as we approach it. When I was younger I was never nervous going into bars, in fact I used to look forward to it every Friday and Saturday night - now however I feel as if I am going into the lion's den.

Strangely Simone is quiet next to me which isn't like her either. Maybe her mask is slipping a bit and she, like me, is actually incredibly nervous at what may lie inside.

Like she said there are two extremely fit guys manning the doors dressed in black suits with white shirts. They are immense, and I swallow hard as I take in their chiselled features and huge muscly bodies straining against the confines of their clothes. Simone draws a deep breath beside me and whistles out in appreciation. She whispers, "I could just stand out here all night and watch them. What I wouldn't give to see them in an underwear campaign for M&S."

I nod in agreement. I am kind of loving this new body craze that is sweeping the land amongst the male species. Suddenly I feel an overwhelming need to join a gym, not for my own fitness levels but for my lust levels. Knowing my luck though it would be full of older men and women desperately trying to

stem the onslaught of old age, myself included!
As we approach I see them looking us up and down
and I am ashamed to admit that I straighten up and
push my almost non existent chest out a little,
thanking God for the invention of the padded bra.
I try to adopt a bored teenageresq pose as if me going
into a bar on a Saturday night is a normal thing.
As we reach them one of them smiles and almost
looks amused. Immediately my worry levels increase
as I wonder what he sees. He must know instantly
that we are novices at this, sad middle aged women
desperately trying to recapture their youth. I almost
blush as sex god number 1 smiles and I note that his
incredibly sexy eyes twinkle as he smiles at us both.
"Evening ladies." Simone smiles seductively at him
and I look at her in surprise. Goodness her a married
woman and all. "Evening guys, room for two more?"
She pushes out her chest and nods towards the bar.
Opening the door he grins. "There's always room for
two such gorgeous women. In you go and you know
where I am if you need me."
He winks which makes me almost faint on the spot.
My fantasies will be in melt down later when I am
back in my bed for one. Fleetingly I wonder if I
should get a single bed now and give myself a bit
more room.
I don't have time to think about re modelling my
room before we are thrust into a whole new world.
Loud music thumps around us and the noise is
deafening. Groups of people all stand around

laughing and drinking and the place is well lit and welcoming. I am actually quite relieved to see that we are not that much out of place here. Yes there are hordes of younger people but there are also many groups of older ones too. I firmly put us in the older bracket and wonder what everyone's story is.

Simone flashes me a grin and I can see the excitement in her eyes. Like me she hasn't done this in a while and I can feel the excitement coming off of her.

We push our way to the bar and order a couple of white wines. By the time we have been served I am starting to relax a little. Nobody has stared at us in amazement yet and we actually blend in quite nicely. We grab our drinks and move away, propping ourselves up in a nearby corner and take in everything around us.

Simone smiles at me happily. "God I've missed this Soph. I've forgotten that there is life after 9pm. Normally I would be ironing or something whilst watching Martin juggle his ipad, phone and remote whilst watching three things simultaneously."

I nod in agreement. "Yes I would probably be thinking about having a bath by now and writing my to do list for tomorrow. I forgot that there is a whole nocturnal world out here."

Simone looks around us and then grins. "Hey look at those guys over there." I turn to look and she hisses. "Don't look round, they'll know we're talking about them and we need to play it cool."

I look at her in amazement. "You said look." She rolls her eyes. "I didn't mean it in the physical sense. No one of them can't take his eyes off you. He looks about our age, a businessman probably on his way home after work. Those guys he is with are probably his office buddies. I must say there is something appealing about him."

I can feel my anxiety levels rising. "Don't be silly Simone; he's not looking at me at all, why on earth would he?"

Simone smiles. "Because you are looking hot tonight. That dress is clinging to your body which isn't half bad for a mars bar munching soda drinking mama whose normal idea of letting her hair down is in the literal sense when she takes her scrunchie out at the end of the day."

I giggle nervously. "I'm sorry Simone but this is all weird. I feel like I'm having an out of body experience. This isn't who I am. I am a mother and soon to be ex wife. Nobody would want me and to be honest I'm not interested in finding anyone anyway." Strange how an image of Daniel suddenly springs to mind. Someone tell my heart that I am not interested in another man because my traitorous heart is not on the same page as the rest of me.

Suddenly Simone stiffens up and says from the corner of her mouth. "Oh my god two of them are coming over."

I look at her in panic. "What! Tell them to keep away, I'm not ready to talk to anyone."

Simone grins. "Yes you are Sophie Bailey. You are ready and furthermore you are going to charm the pants off that guy because Lysander is not the only one who can attract attention. You need a bit of gentle flirting for your own self esteem. Squash those fears down and live for the moment. There's a new girl in town and she is taking no prisoners."

I don't have time to answer before the guys reach us. I notice that they look about our age and like Simone said look as though they have just stepped out of the office. Both seem quite attractive and one of them looks me up and down and then grins.

"Hi ladies, sorry to descend on you both like this but we haven't seen you here before and wanted to welcome you personally."

I smile nervously and Simone just says, "Hi yourselves. I'm Chantelle and this is Winona."

Oh not those two again! I look at Simone and raise my eyes as she grins at me.

The guy who spoke says, "I'm Chris and this is Steve." He fixes me with what I am sure that he thinks is a sexy look but quite frankly he isn't doing it for me. There is something quite predatory about him and his smile doesn't reach his eyes.

He says softly, "Well Winona why don't you tell me more about yourself?" I notice that Steve pulls Simone to one side and is talking to her so I just take a deep breath and put my game face on.

"There's nothing much to tell really. I don't live far from here and for some strange reason I am suddenly foot loose and fancy free after my husband traded me in for a younger model."

I know that it goes against every rule to lay everything out in the open like this but I don't care. I'm not interested in this man and hopefully I can just put him off me by being honest. I mean I'm hardly catch of the day am I?

To my surprise his eyes light up and he leans forward and whispers. "Then your husband is a fool. If you were my wife I wouldn't let you out of my sight for a minute."

I take a large gulp of wine and feel actually quite happy to hear his words. It's been a while since somebody paid me attention and made me feel desirable. Maybe Mimi and Simone are right, this is just what I need.

I smile at Chris and decide to give him a chance. "So Chris, tell me your story." He looks at me with an intense expression and his eyes hold mine as he says softly. "I am like you foot loose and fancy free and I work hard and play even harder. I have just come from the office and was just intending to have a few drinks before heading home to my bachelor pad for one. Now I have found you though Winona I very much want to stay and see where this chance encounter will take us."

I swallow hard as I see him rake every inch of my body with his intense eyes. He shifts closer until he is inches from me and I feel the heat of his body. Suddenly it is as though we are alone in the bar. The music fades into the background and the chattering dies down in my mind. All I can hear is my own heart thumping as the man in front of me devours me with his eyes.

He leans in and whispers, "We could be so good together baby. One thing you need to know about me is that I appreciate a good thing when I see it and that my darling is you. What do you say; would you like to have dinner with me tonight?"

I swallow nervously. "Um that sounds lovely but I am with my friend, maybe some other time."

He shifts even closer and his hand brushes against mine. Leaning down he whispers, "I want you Winona, I want to feel your sexy body against every part of me. I want to cover every inch of you with my mouth and give you pleasure beyond your wildest dreams. I want to keep you tied up in my bed all night and all day and hear you screaming my name as I send you over the edge as I fuck you hard."

He shifts until his body is pressing against me and I can feel how hard he is as I spit my drink in his face in shock.

He jumps back, "What the hell?" Flustered I try to help mop up the wine that is dripping down his face. "I'm so sorry I really didn't mean to do that, I was just taken by surprise that's all."

Frantically I look around me for some napkins or something to clear up the mess and look at him in despair. Taking a handkerchief out of his pocket he mops up the liquid and looks at me with frustration.

I see Simone looking at us in shock and I just babble on apologetically. "I'm so sorry; you just shocked me a bit if I'm honest. I didn't mean to do that." He steps back and I see the evidence of my shock staining his once immaculate grey suit. Steve looks over and I see the laughter in his eyes. Chris just looks at me and then appears to re-group. Leaning in he reaches up and tucks a stray piece of hair behind my ear as he whispers, "You know you could always make it up to me. Why don't you come home with me and clear up this mess with your tongue?" Suddenly I feel violated. This isn't right. Nobody has ever spoken to me like this before and I am actually not ok with it. This guy is now seriously creeping me out and I need to get away from him fast.

I look at him and just smile sadly. "I wish that I could baby. You are right we could be so good together. I would like nothing more than to give you what you so obviously deserve but the trouble is my husband left me for much more of a reason than I told you about." I can see the excitement in his eyes as he takes in my words and then I watch it leave his eyes like a bat out of hell when I say, "You see I told him that I wanted children. Lots of them, a whole football team. I am shall we say primed and ready for action and the first man that fucks me hard as you so nicely put it will be getting more than just the fuck of his life, he will be getting a whole new family because when I drop my knickers it's with one aim in mind, procreation."

He moves away as though I have given him an electric shock. Panic fills his eyes and he looks around him wildly.

I fix him with my best crazy bitch face and he steps back and coughs nervously.

"Anyway ladies, it's been good to meet you both but I'm afraid I have a prior engagement that I can't get out of. Maybe we will see you around." He turns to his friend. "Sorry Steve got to go. See you on Monday."

We watch as he leaves as fast as a Formula One car off the grid and Simone and Steve look at me in shock. "What was that all about?" I grin.

"Oh I don't know, maybe something came up."

Chapter Twenty Two

We laugh about what happened all the way home.
Simone couldn't believe what Chris had said to me
and was even more surprised that I didn't take him up
on his kind offer.

She drops me off. "I had fun tonight Soph. You know
I'm sure that all men aren't like Chris. He was
probably a one off. Don't let that experience put you
off trying again. I'm sure there are perfectly
respectable men out there looking for love the same
as you."

I look at her and smile weakly. "The trouble is
Simone I'm not looking for love. I thought I had
found it with Lysander and to tell you the truth I'm
just not interested in replacing him just yet. It's
actually the last thing on my mind. All I want is to
wake up and for this to all have been a terrible
nightmare. I had the perfect life or so I thought and it
is too soon to look for a new one. No, I'm just better
off learning the Xbox and leaving the dating scene
well alone."

Simone smiles at me as I open the car door. "You'll
be fine Soph. You're right it's probably too soon to
think beyond tomorrow but there will come a time
when you realise that it actually doesn't hurt
anymore. You will recover from this you know, it
just may take a little bit of time."

I smile and say goodnight. As I walk up the path to

my little cottage I dread going inside. It isn't home anymore, just a place where my memories haunt me every hour of every day. Perhaps it is time to move on, start again and try to move forward. The trouble is the thought of it is breaking my heart all over again.

For the first time in forever I actually get a lie in. Even Mr Tumnus decides to sleep in and I wake up at 10am with just the sound of the birds outside for company. I reach over and stroke my puppy's soft furry ears. I decided that Mr Tumnus could sleep with me from now on. Lysander never wanted him in the bedroom but he doesn't get a say anymore. In fact it gives me perverse pleasure to think that he would be horrified to know that he now sleeps where he used to.

I decide to have a lazy day whilst I can. It is very rare for me to have a day to myself and I decide to waste it in a purely selfish way. I stay in my pyjamas and watch a film about aliens in space before donning my old track suit to take Mr Tumnus out for a very long walk. I am actually quite enjoying my own company and realise that this is the first time that I haven't been racing around after my two boys worrying about ironing and making the Sunday roast. In fact I may even just grab a frozen pizza out of the oven and watch another film with a bottle of wine.

The afternoon goes quickly as I get Harry's uniform ready for school tomorrow and try to piece together an outfit for my first day at work in a very long time. I finally decide on a smart blue dress that I bought for £5 in the H&M sale. You actually can't beat the sales and the feeling when you grab such a bargain is better than sex. Ok maybe it's time to buy a kindle. Obviously I have been missing out on this new sexual revolution and I am kind of curious as to what I have been missing out on.

Lysander and I had been a once a week if we were lucky kind of couple. We sort of fell into a routine which I was happy with even if as it turns out he wasn't. To tell you the truth he was always the last thing on my to do list.

Finally the dreaded hour approaches when I will have to see him again and I steel myself for it.

As expected dead on 7pm the doorbell rings. Lysander has always been punctual and it caused many an argument between us because punctuality has never been my forte.

I open the door and a little tornado sweeps into the room, right past me to Mr Tumnus. Lysander follows him in and stands awkwardly in the doorway.

He nods his head curtly.

"Well here we are safe and sound as promised." He thrusts Harry's bag towards me and I nod saying, "Thanks, don't let me keep you."

He looks surprised and then smiles sadly. "I am sorry you know Sophie, I never meant to hurt you. You were a good wife to me and don't deserve all of this, but what was I to do, I couldn't go on living a lie it wasn't fair on any of us?"

I look at him angrily and keep my voice low so that Harry can't hear us. "A little warning would have been nice; oh I don't know some sort of sign. I can understand why you have done this but I cannot understand why you didn't even try to make it work. If only you had told me then we could have worked at it, I don't know gone for counselling or something. Instead you just made up your mind and that was that. Don't start saying sorry now because it just won't cut it. I'm just sorry that you are not the man I thought you were. Now if you don't mind I have a son to take care of."

Lysander looks at me with a frozen expression and then just turns and leaves and I slam the door shut behind him.

Chapter Twenty Three

Ok deep breaths and try not to hyperventilate. This is it, my first job in many years and I am feeling extremely nervous.

I had to get up super early to walk Mr Tumnus and practically ran around the fields dragging a very sleepy disgruntled little boy behind me.

By the time we set off for the short journey I feel as if I have been up for hours already.

I feel a bit guilty about leaving Mr Tumnus home alone and promise him that I will pop home for lunch and take him for a walk. Six hours is just too long to leave him on his own and I am actually feeling sick at the thought of it. Will I ever have nothing to feel guilty about?

Harry chatters all the way and is very excited that his mummy is going with him to school. I hold his little hand in mine and thank God that I have him in my life. I know that it will be a very short amount of time that he will enjoy spending time with me and is proud that I will be at school and not embarrassed by it. It won't be long before he doesn't say two words to me and spends all of his time in his room on some computer game or another. He won't want his mum hanging around him then and until that dreaded day I am going to make the most of every minute that I am the most important person in his life.

Luckily we are able to go in early so I will be spared

the mafia inquisition. In fact come to think of it I have got away with it all quite lightly so far. Even Annabelle was more intent on getting to her country club function rather than interrogate me about my situation. Mind you the subject probably bores her; I mean I'm not exactly that interesting after all.

As we push our way into the school playground my nerves increase. I feel like it's my first day at school all over again which is stupid when you come to think of it. It feels strange to be the only ones here and that in just a few short minutes the place will fill up with hordes of screaming children and their scary mums.

With a deep breath we go through the hallowed door into the reception area.

Harry must also feel strange because he grips my hand tightly as I call out, "Hi, Um Mr Rainford its Sophie and Harry."

My voice sounds weak and nervous and I give myself a stern talking to within. Toughen up Sophie Bailey you're an independent working woman now grow a backbone.

My breath catches as the wondrous sight of Daniel fills the doorway. He stands there smiling at us and his eyes have a way of drawing you in and making you feel as if you are the only person in the room. Ok I am the only person in the room - get a grip.

"Hi Sophie," he smiles before turning to Harry. "And hi you too little buddy. Do you want to give me a hand in the classroom whilst your mummy settles into her office?"

MY OFFICE! Harry nods enthusiastically and runs off in excitement. Daniel winks at me and I almost pass out on the spot. "I'll just give him something to keep him occupied and then I'll be back to sort you out."

As he follows my son I allow myself a few moments to envisage exactly how I want him to - sort me out! I walk into my new office and stare around me with complete and utter terror. There will be no hiding here. I have to be good at this because I don't want to let Daniel, Harry or myself down. It's time to stand up and be counted.

I sit down at the desk and look at the piles of notes in front of me. Mrs Fletcher has left me various instructions and a to do checklist. Gosh a woman after my own heart. I need a to do list just to get up these days.

My heart jumps as Daniel comes into the room and stares at me with his sexy eyes. I can feel a flush creeping over my body as I see his body straining against the confines of his clothes. I notice the way that his eyes sparkle and his hair has that- *just got out of bed style*- that us women love.

"Well Sophie Bailey are you ready for this?" I nod and smile weakly. He looks at me for a few seconds and I can't tear my eyes away from him. I mean he is totally gorgeous after all.

He sits down on the corner of my desk and I swallow hard.

"So how have you been, has it all sunk in yet?"
I shake my head sadly. "Not really but it will have to soon because my life is suddenly going at a million miles an hour and I will have to keep up if I stand any chance of getting through this."
He nods. "How did it go with your solicitor?" I shrug. "As well as can be expected I suppose. She seems perfectly capable and I am happy to let her take charge."
We are interrupted as we hear the sounds of the others arriving outside and Daniel grins. "Well now it begins. You and me against the mafia, working together side by side trying to exist in a hostile environment."
I snort and then feel the waves of mortification sweep over me- did I just SNORT again?
Trying to divert his attention away from my acute embarrassment I just wave my hand towards the playground.
"You will be fine Daniel, me on the other hand - well lets just say I'm about to become public enemy number one out there."
He looks surprised. "Why?"
I giggle. "Because I get to work in here with you." He studies me for a moment and then just smiles before heading off to do whatever it is that teachers do before their day is filled with tears and tantrums. Now I am alone and with great determination start reading through every one of Mrs Fletcher's notes.

The morning passes by in a flash. I am surprised how quickly I settle in and am happy to discover that Mrs Fletcher is apparently quite similar to me in how she works. Everything is in good order and easy to find and there appears to be a checklist for everything. I actually feel as if I am in love with her by morning break.

I hear the children stampeding towards the playground and then as the door opens my heart lurches as I see Daniel leaning against the doorframe looking sexily at me.

"Well Mrs Bailey, how are things in the land of lists and filing?"

I grin. "Very organised and easy to follow actually."

Daniel smiles. "Well let me buy my newest staff member a much needed coffee to reward her for her hard work so far. You probably could do with it and I know that I could as the natives have been extremely restless this morning."

I laugh and he smiles at me softly. "That's better Sophie, that's what we need to see more of - you laughing. In fact I am going to make it my personal mission to wipe that worried look from your face at every opportunity."

He holds out his hand and my heart almost stops beating as I allow him to pull me up from my chair. As our hands touch I feel a shiver of desire run through me. Instantly I admonish myself. Get a grip Sophie, you're all over the place and he is only being kind!

We walk towards the staff room and I decide to do a bit of digging and find out as much as I can about him.

"So tell me Daniel do you live far?"

He smiles. "The other side of town. It's quite convenient and everything we need is on our doorstep."

My heart plunges as he says we. Of course he lives with someone. It would be against the law for him to live alone.

"Oh, that's nice. Have you lived there long?"

He nods. "About a year. It was a new development and actually provided us with everything that we needed, no decorating to do, all mod cons and close proximity to everything we need. The price wasn't too bad either."

I have to know more about this "we" so press on.

"You say us, how many of you live there?" He laughs. "You make it sound like a squat."

I feel embarrassed and as we reach the staffroom door he stops with his hand on the handle and looks at me with a soft smile on his heavenly lips.

"Sorry that sounded a bit rude. There are only two of us. We have been friends for years and then decided to take the plunge and live together. His name is Sam and he is a pilot."

He opens the door and all of my hopes and fantasies come crashing down. I was right, of course he is gay. No normal man dresses like he does and has impeccable grooming. He is also in touch with his feminine side and the concern and friendly banter is just even more evidence. My gaydar is spot on and at this moment in time I am devastated to be proved right.

As we head inside I look with interest around me. The staffroom is a small room with a comfy settee and a little kitchen area. The only other people in here are Miss Barley and Mrs Sims who are chatting together on the other side of the room. As we come in they look up and smile warmly.

Miss Barley smiles. "Hi Sophie, how's it going?" I smile back at them and nod. "Great thank you; I'm actually quite surprised how quickly I've settled in." They both smile and then I notice Daniel thrusting a large steaming mug of coffee at me. "Here you go, just what the doctor ordered. Do you fancy a biscuit with that?"

Thinking that what I fancy more is him I quickly try to push the thoughts away. He is now going to have to be my gay best friend because I absolutely cannot allow myself to think of him in any other way. God life is so unfair, why are all the best ones gay?

We sit down and I try not to let the feel of his leg against mine affect me. I try to picture Daniel as Elton John to distract my thoughts. I could use George Michael but as I always had a crush on him too it wouldn't help the situation.

Daniel chatters on about the school and tries to answer any questions that I have and soon the small amount of time that we have passes and we reluctantly head back to our relevant jobs.

Once I am back in my office I carry on with my job which involves stuffing envelopes with letters informing the parents of the impending parents evening.

I must get quite involved in my task because when the phone rings it makes me almost jump out of my skin.

"Fairdale Infant school, how may I help you?"

Gosh I sound very professional and in charge.

"Soph is that you?"

I hear the unmistakeable voice of Simone and breathe a sigh of relief.

"Yes how are you Simone?"

"Fine, just checking in on the worker. How many times have you had sex with Mr Rainford already?"

I giggle and then blush looking around me as if everyone can hear us.

"Shut up Simone I told you I'm not having sex with anyone and the only X in my life at the moment ends with box, unless you count my lying cheating soon to be ex husband."

Simone laughs.

"You say that now but my bet is that if he so much as hinted at a quick one before lunch is out you would be dropping those knickers quicker than you could jump him."

Despite myself I laugh. "Shut up Simone I've told you he's gay. He just looks on me as a friend in need."

She snorts. "More like needy. Anyway how do you know he's gay?"

"He good as told me. He lives with another man and they are really happy."

Simone sounds disappointed. "God life is so unfair. Why are the best ones always gay? When I found out about Ricky Martin I cried for a week. Maybe you should have taken creepy Chris up on his offer on Saturday night. He was a creep but you could have used him for sex."

I shudder. "Listen I am using nobody for sex and especially not some creepy guy who spoke to me so crudely moments after meeting me in some pick up joint of a bar. Anyway I have to go, some of us have work to do after all."

"Ok have it your way but I am going to spend the afternoon drafting out your online profile for Tinder."

I shriek. "Don't you dare, I very much do not need an online profile and definitely not for a dating website. Go and knit Martin a jumper or something instead. I'll see you later."

Shaking my head I put down the phone and smile to myself. Simone is incorrigible.

Suddenly I am aware that I am not alone and as I look up I see the most gorgeous example of manhood staring at me with an extremely amused expression on his devastatingly handsome face.

Chapter Twenty Four

Just for a moment I think I forget to breathe. This man in front of me is super super hot and I am looking at every fantasy figure in my head rolled into one. He has dirty blonde hair that is spiked and messy. His eyes are the brightest green and he has a strong jaw line showing off perfectly white teeth. His skin is tanned and he is wearing black jeans with a brown suede jacket. His body looks amazing underneath the T Shirt that clings to a muscular body. He smiles at me and then laughs out loud.

"You must be Sophie, I'm Sam and I'm very pleased to meet you."

Ok major disappointment, world coming crashing down and I think I'm going to cry. This must be Daniel's boyfriend.

Trying to recover I just smile. "I'm pleased to meet you too Sam, Daniel has told me a little bit about you and I know that you live together."

He winks and then holds up a Tupperware container. "Dan forgot his lunch and you really don't want to be around him if he's hungry. There's only so many biscuits a man can take before he is driven sugar overload mad."

I stand up and take the lunch box from him.

"It's very good of you to drop it over Sam. Daniel said that you live on the other side of town, it must have been a bit out of your way."

Sam just grins and lowers his voice.

"To tell you the truth Sophie he would rather I didn't come anywhere near this place."

I look at him in surprise and he whispers,

"He's quite a private person you know and doesn't like his private life interfering with his public one if you know what I mean."

I nod trying extremely hard to mask my disappointed face. Life is so cruel. These two men are absolute perfection and are so off the market.

Sam grins. "Anyway what about you? Daniel tells me that you're going through a tough time at the moment. I must admit that it sounds like you've got everything under control judging by the conversation I just overheard."

I blush and then grin as I catch his eye. Suddenly we are laughing like school children and I have to see the funny side otherwise I would dissolve into a blubbering heap.

Sam comes and sits down opposite me and I will myself not to stare at him.

"So Sophie what was that all about? By the sounds of it you had a nasty encounter with some creepy guy in a bar, come on tell all."

I grin at him and find myself telling him every last sorry detail. I don't know why but he is so easy to talk to and I can see my future with the two of them. I will be their female best friend and we will be the fearsome threesome and I will accompany them to gay bars and watch Judy Garland films.

Yes this is my future and I am actually more than happy about it.

Sam laughs when I finish and then his eyes twinkle mischievously. "That sounds like fun. Maybe I could come out with you next time. I can't say my evenings are as exciting as yours, perhaps I'm going to the wrong places."

I laugh and smile at him warmly. "Of course you're welcome Sam, both of you are. However my evenings out will have to be put on hold until I master the art of the Xbox."

Sam looks confused and I fill him in on the details. Once again he laughs out loud. "Your solicitor sounds awesome. She's right though, Xbox is kind of addictive. I could show you how it all works if you like. I'm away tomorrow for a week but when I get back we'll set a date for the lesson in combat and pulverisation."

Looking at him surprise I manage to stutter, "What about Daniel, will he mind? I mean he doesn't like to mix private with public."

Sam grins wickedly. "He doesn't need to know. He's not my keeper and after all it's all perfectly innocent anyway."

I nod but feel a little bit bad. For some reason it doesn't feel right not telling him and now I have major anxiety.

Sam laughs. "Just kidding Soph you should see your face. He can come if he likes and we'll all play. Trouble is Daniel isn't much of a game player, I'm trying to teach him in the art of that along with several other things if you know what I mean."

I blush and look down. Goodness Sam is a bit full on. No wonder Daniel likes to keep him away from our sleepy village.

Suddenly Sam stands up and moves towards the door. "Listen I had better not keep you from your work. My mission is accomplished and now I have to get home to pack. Now remember we have a date and tell Dan if you like, he can join us if he wants to. Oh but only if it's ok with you?"

He winks and I smile at him. "Great, I'll get the beers in and we'll make an evening of it. Have a good trip, are you going anywhere nice?"

"Yes Australia, it's a gutsy trip but not a bad one really. We get a few days there and it will be good to get some sun even if it is only for a few days."

I nod in agreement. "Yes the only sun I get these days is the newspaper." Sam laughs out loud.

"Sophie Bailey if you are a Sun reader then I read Woman's Own"

I grin. "Well maybe we can swap them from time to time."

Sam laughs and then says gently. "I can see why Dan likes you so much Soph. You are everything he described and more. I am very much going to enjoy getting to know you Sophie Bailey, are you ready for that?"

I laugh. "Ready as I'll ever be, but I'm not sure that you are ready for me. My life is a bit crazy at the moment and I am liable to do some very strange things."

As he opens the door he winks. "Promises promises. Now I must be off, bon voyage Sophie, stay away from bars and creepy guys until I return. You may want to knit me a jumper in my absence to keep you out of trouble."

Before I can reply he leaves and for some strange reason I can't stop smiling.

Chapter Twenty Five

Lunch time comes and Daniel comes in and groans.
I look at him and smile softly. "Tough day?"
He shakes his head. "Not really but I forgot my lunch
this morning and now I'll have to go and drive to the
nearest petrol station to grab something."
I laugh and hold aloft his lunch box.
"Is this what you forgot?"
He looks at me in complete surprise. "How did you
get that?"
I smile. "Sam brought it in after morning break."
Daniel suddenly looks worried and I can see that he
isn't happy about it in the slightest.
"What Sam was here?" I smile softly.
"Yes but he didn't stay long as he is off on a trip. He
seems nice though."
Daniel looks at me with a hard expression.
"Oh yes Sam is extremely nice. The trouble is he
shouldn't have come here lunch or no lunch."
I look at him in surprise and he notices my
expression and his face softens.
"I'm sorry Sophie you must think me so odd. Of
course it was good of him to bring the lunch. I'll
make sure to tell him just how good of him I thought
it was. Anyway don't you have a dog to walk?"
Suddenly my guilt comes rushing back.
"Oh my god, poor Mr Tumnus he must have his legs
crossed."

Daniel laughs. "Mr Tumnus hey, strange name for a dog."

I grin. "Harry's idea. It was his favourite book when we got the puppy and he thought that he needed a good friend the same as the children in the Lion the Witch and The Wardrobe. Voila Mr Tumnus was named and they have been inseparable ever since."

Daniel grins.

"Good story." I laugh.

"What the book or the puppy?"

He laughs. "Both."

Suddenly he looks more serious. "Listen Sophie if it's easier for you why don't you start a little later so that you can walk Mr Tumnus after dropping Harry to school. We can be flexible here and I don't like to think of you having to rush to walk the dog as well as get a small child ready. It will be dark early soon and it doesn't seem right for you to have to walk them both in the dark."

My eyes fill up and he looks at me in alarm. Smiling through my tears I just say, "Thank you Daniel. I'm sorry I'm such a bad mess at the moment. It's just that any hint of kindness sends me over the edge."

He laughs softly. "Well I can be mean if you like."

I smile. "No you're just fine as you are. Thank you. Now I had better hurry. Oh and another thing, don't worry if you leave your lunch in future. I could always grab you something from home if you're stuck, it's the least I could do after you have been so fantastic."

I notice a strange look flash across his face as I speak and then he just smiles softly.

"I find it very easy to be fantastic around you Sophie Bailey."

I roll my eyes and grab my bag and just smile happily at him as I leave him to it.

I think about everything that happened this morning as I walk Mr Tumnus through the fields. Despite my disappointment at having my suspicions confirmed regarding Daniel I am actually really happy to have met Sam. He was so much fun and I felt at ease with him almost immediately.

I am also really enjoying my new job. It's been so long since I actually had one that I'm not going to lie I was quite nervous about taking it on. I'm glad that I did now, I mean there are only so many times you can clean the house.

The hour passes quickly and I just have time to finish the walk and grab a quick sandwich before I am due back to work. Once again I feel guilty at leaving Mr Tumnus and resolve to make it up to him later.

The afternoon flies by amid a mountain of envelopes, filing and answering the phone.

The other teachers seem nice despite the fact that there are only two teachers and two teaching assistants in the whole school. I mean as village schools go this has got to be one of the smallest. We don't even have a head teacher as such; we just share the one from the other school in the neighbouring village - a sort of Head share. Even she is nice, Mrs Rowley is her name and she appears to spend the majority of her time in the other school, apparently content to hand over the reigns to Mr Rainford in her absence, hence my appointment.

To my disappointment I don't see much of Daniel for the rest of the day. He is very busy and all I get is the odd glimpse of him in the distance.

Soon the final bell rings and I join the other mothers outside in the playground.

I can feel the curious stares all around me. I stand in my usual place and wait for Simone to join me. She is obviously running late and I silently pray for her to hurry up. Then I see Annabelle Buckley bearing down on me with a determined look on her face.

"Sophie, darling I missed you this morning how are things?"

I can feel the interested looks all around me and paste a bright smile on my face.

"I'm fine thank you Annabelle, how are you?"

She does that sort of smile that almost looks like a grimace and waves her hand. "Oh you know busy busy as usual, there just aren't enough hours in the day."

I nod in agreement as she continues.

"Thank you for your help on Saturday I hope that I can count on you this one too."

I feel her eyes piercing me and fleetingly wonder why it is so important to her. I just nod.

"Yes no problem. Is 10am still ok?"

She looks almost relieved and just nods. "Super darling, I'll tell the kids that you're coming. Daisy will be so pleased especially if you bring Harry." She laughs shrilly. "I think she has a bit of a crush on him you know, almost as big as the one you have on our glorious teacher, but then again maybe not that big hey?" She winks at me and I can feel the ears straining to hear every word around us. Feeling myself blush I say in shock, "I'm sorry Annabelle but you must be mistaken. I most certainly do not have a crush on Mr Rainford; I don't know where you get that from."

Annabelle just winks and looks at me knowingly before turning to leave. As she does so she says over her shoulder, "Just keep on telling yourself that darling, but you cannot lie to yourself."

As I look at her retreating figure leaving me in complete shock I am aware of Simone racing up and panting beside me. "God I thought I'd miss the bell. I couldn't put my latest book down and now I'm all of a fluster in more ways than one."

I look at her in total shock not really registering her words.

"Simone do you think I have a crush on Mr Rainford? I mean surely it's no more than anyone else here, why does everyone think that there's something more when it comes to me?"

Simone looks worried. "I've heard the whispers Sophie. Word is that you have a major crush on our delightful love god and Lysander found out. You apparently have been arguing about it for months and he finally snapped and left you, citing your unhealthy obsession on our drop gorgeous teacher as the catalyst. The fact that you have now supposedly engineered two after school liaisons with him and wormed your way into Mrs Fletcher's old job is even more proof. Many are saying that you had something on her which is why she was forced to take early retirement to vacate her job to you."

I look at my friend and the words don't come. I open my mouth and then close it again for once totally speechless.

Simone laughs. "Mad aren't they? You can tell that we live in a small village. Things are so boring they have to fabricate the gossip. Don't worry though it will all blow over. They are probably just jealous that you are having all the fun."

The tears spring to my eyes and I lean back against the wall. "Fun you say, I can assure you that none of this is fun. There is no fun at all on being abandoned by the person you love and then suddenly having to worry about everything, especially after not having a worry in the world. I am fast approaching middle age with only my son to show for it. My future is probably as a single mother tucked away in a shared flat somewhere scratching a living to get by getting my kicks from random men chatting me up in bars trying to get into my knickers.

The only food I will be able to eat is what I can forage from the land because they don't sell much food in poundland and that is all I can afford. I'm sorry Simone but none of this is fun and if I could I would take my lying, cheating, weak husband back in a heartbeat because despite everything that has happened I still love him and my heart has broken into a million pieces."

Simone reaches out and hugs me to her as I feel the tears splashing on to her shoulder. I want to cry like a baby but am mindful of where I am. These women would revel in my misery and delight in my impending madness. They are only happy if someone is worse off than them because then it makes sense of their own lives. They can take the moral high ground and bask in the knowledge that their lives unlike mine are perfect. The fact that they are probably anything but doesn't matter. They work along the lines that if they know someone that bad things are happening to then the chances are it wouldn't happen to them.

This is my life now, the subject of whispers and rumour and there is not a thing I can do about it.

Chapter Twenty Six

I decide to spend the evening focusing on the two most important people in my life and go for a long walk with Harry and Mr Tumnus.

As we head through the woods I shake the trees to enable Harry to catch the falling leaves.

We play hide and seek and pooh sticks over the little stream and hearing Harry's excited screams of delight and laughter is all I need to hear. We might be going through the most devastating thing that has happened to us as a family but I know that we will be alright. I will make sure of it.

The rest of the evening is spent making chocolate cookies and watching one of Harry's DVDs. I am feeling in a Disney mood again and manage to persuade him to watch The Pirates of the Caribbean. He falls asleep on my lap and as I stoke his hair and feel Mr Tumnus's warm furry body curled up beside us I realise that everything I need is here in this room.

I will ignore the gossip and push down the hurt that I am feeling. From now on I will be Super Mum and no challenge will be too great.

Soon Harry is tucked up in bed and I decide to run a bath. I feel tired after my full on day and am looking forward to an early night. As I sink into the hot sweet smelling water the phone rings.

Cursing I jump out, the water splashing everywhere as I grab the towel off the radiator. Typical couldn't they have rung two minutes earlier, if that's one of those sales calls I won't be held responsible for the language that will spill from my lips.

I almost wish it had been when I hear Lysander bellowing into the phone.

"You total bitch Sophie. How dare you get your solicitor to send me a letter citing my supposed adultery. We were going to divorce on the grounds of irreconcilable differences and you just had to turn nasty didn't you? Ocean is beside herself at being dragged into this and has had to go to a retreat to deal with her damaged aura. Why have you done this? It's not as if I haven't been anything but good to you throughout it all."

I listen to his tirade in shock. He must be seriously delusional if he thinks that I am being a bitch in all of this. I can feel the anger building up inside me and mindful of Harry sleeping in the next room I keep my voice low and controlled, despite the fact that I am anything but.

"Firstly Lysander we agreed to nothing, you decided that was going to be the reason. The facts are that you did leave me for somebody else so deal with it. Secondly I couldn't give a toss about your girlfriend's damaged aura because quite frankly you have smashed mine into a million pieces and the saying if you play with fire you get burnt springs to mind. Maybe she might just realise what she has done in stealing my husband from me and breaking up a once happy family. You don't get away with treating this whole situation as if it is just something that needs dealing with like taking out the trash before you carry on with your new perfect life. I will not be swept under the carpet and you are going to have to face the consequences of your actions. I am going to get the best divorce I can from you because it is all I have got now and I have to secure the best future for my child. So suck it up baby and accept the inevitable because I am not the pushover you think I am."

Phew I feel quite proud of myself. It is as though I am in the wild west squaring up to an opponent, pistols drawn. I have even adopted a stance as I speak and wonder what the neighbours would say if they could see me draped in a towel taking on the baddie in all my gladiator glory.

Lysander lowers his voice and snarls through the phone. "Have it your way bitch but you will never win. All you have done is turn this ugly and I am coming for you. Enjoy living in that house because soon you will have to move out. I am only paying for the mortgage and the minimum amount that I have to from now on. You are about to find out that you are no longer on the gravy train and money is going to be extremely tight from now on. Enjoy finding ways to pay for your fancy solicitor because you are about to be cut off. Two can play at this game and you will find that I hold all the cards. I will be picking Harry up on Friday night as before and bringing him back on Sunday. Until then I will be doing everything I can to cut you out of my life, so enjoy your small victories whilst you can because I am going to win this war. By the time I finish with you there will be nothing left."

He slams the phone down and I am left reeling. The tears once again spring to my eyes and I can feel my heart thumping frantically in my chest. What have I done? I'm not strong enough for this despite my brave words. As I sink back into my now luke warm bath I come to the realisation that I am seriously screwed.

Chapter Twenty Seven

For the next few days I exist on autopilot. I try not to talk about my situation even to Simone as every time I think about it I want to bawl out in hysterics. How on earth did my life spiral out of control so badly? I even try to dodge Daniel, I know it shouldn't have but the rumours have got to me. What if he thinks I am stalking him? He has been so kind to me and the fact that he is gay probably explains away his compassionate side.

I don't want to cause him any more trouble so just keep out of his way and the brief times that we do spend together I just act all businesslike and busy. I can tell that he is surprised by my almost coldness but I can't drag him into the lies and gossip. No it's for the best. I need to focus on Harry and become a strong stable mother for all our sakes.

So that is how it is, I am now robo mum. I put everything into my child and my home and try to do the best job that I can. By the time Friday comes around I am mentally exhausted and completely dreading seeing Lysander tonight when he picks Harry up.

Just before the final bell I am surprised to see Daniel appear in the office. I am even more surprised when he walks in purposefully and closes the door behind him. Sitting down in the chair opposite he fixes me with a hard stare.

"Right then Sophie, what's happening? You've been avoiding me all week and I want to know what happened to make you distance yourself like this." To say I am shocked is putting it mildly. He is looking at me with a strange mixture of hurt and anger and I can't quite believe it. I just shrug and say quietly.

"I'm sorry Daniel but things have got a bit out of hand this week so I am retreating into myself a bit. It's not you, of course it isn't as you have been so kind to me."

I lift my eyes and look into his. "I heard certain rumours that surprised me a bit. I mean I know that the mafia is relentless but they even shocked me." He looks surprised. "What rumours are they?"

I proceed to tell him what was said and I am surprised when his face relaxes and he laughs softly. "Gosh those mothers should write a screenplay; their imagination is off the scale." Despite myself I grin at him and his eyes soften and he smiles softly at me.

"Carry on Sophie; I can't believe that you would let them affect you this much, has something else happened?"

I shake my head sadly and tell him about my run in with Lysander. As I look at him his expression hardens and his eyes turn almost black with anger. "I can see why you have been somewhat pre-occupied. You shouldn't have to deal with all of this on your own. Is there anyone who could come and stay with you for a bit to help you?"

I shake my head. "No, I told you it's only me and my parents live in Spain. To tell you the truth they don't even know yet. I'm sort of dreading telling them because they love Lysander and always thought that he was too good for me."

Daniel looks shocked. "Why would they think that, you're their daughter for god's sake?"

I shrug. "I've always been a disappointment to them. They always wanted a boy and used to tell me that at every given opportunity. They also wanted me to become a hot shot accountant or something and I never really measured up to their vision for my future. The fact that I married and became a housewife just re-enforces their opinion of me. Lysander on the other hand can do no wrong in their eyes. He is successful and was a good husband. He is also a boy and he replaced me extremely quickly in their affections when he came along. The fact that they live in Spain is a god send really because I get to pretend that they don't exist for most of the year."

Daniel leans across the desk and takes my hand in his which makes my stomach flip at the contact and says softly, "I'm sorry Sophie; I can't believe that anyone wouldn't be more than happy than to have you as a wife and a daughter. They don't know how wrong they are. You are not only a beautiful, kind and funny woman but the perfect mother to Harry. Your qualities exist way outside those of a corporate hound and the fact that your parents can't see that is their loss. Your husband is a fool and don't let the mafia get you down. They are obviously jealous of you and you should just be flattered to be the subject of their speculation. So stand tall Sophie Bailey and be proud of who you are. In the end you are a strong beautiful woman who could have it all if you wanted."

He squeezes my hand and I look at him and smile. He grins. "That's better. Now no more hiding yourself away. I missed my new friend this week and now we have to make up for it."

I look at him in surprise. "What do you mean?" He laughs. Sam told me about your wish to learn the Xbox and we as it happens are experts. With me being a teacher and all I think I could have you rather good at it by the end of the weekend."

Ok there is now definitely a god because he must have sent Daniel and Sam to me as my guardian Angels. He jumps up.

"Now we've got that out of the way I'll be round at 8pm. That should give you enough time to deal with your husband's visit and chill the beers. I hope you're a fast learner Sophie because you will have to be to keep up with me."

As I watch him leave I am suddenly very much looking forward to the weekend.

Chapter Twenty Eight

I head home as if on auto pilot. I can't believe that I am spending the evening with Daniel and even Lysander's impending visit does nothing to dampen my spirits.

I make Harry some tea and pack his weekend bag. I absolutely hate and detest the thought that he will be away from me even for one night let alone two. I am just so grateful to Daniel for rescuing me from a night of solitude which would inevitably end up with me cracking open a bottle of wine and sitting crying into it for the rest of the night as I wave goodbye to my hopes and dreams as they head off to their new life on the Ocean waves. I actually now hate Ocean with a passion. In my mind she has totally woven a spell to trap Lysander and in my mind I picture her as a witch. I can only hope that she is still repairing her damaged aura because the thought of her getting her claws into my son as well is too much to bear.

The dreaded hour approaches and I hear Lysander's car pulling up outside.

Harry is beyond excited and it is only the thought that he loves his father and enjoys spending time with him that allows me to relinquish him to his care. Is it wrong of me to wish that Harry couldn't stand him and would cling to my legs howling for me not to let the bad man take him?

No such luck and Harry screams with delight as he

flings himself on to his father. Lysander just nods to me and without saying a word takes Harry's bag in one hand and him in the other and walks away.

For a moment I watch them go and it tugs at my heartstrings as Harry waves at me excitedly from the front seat of the car and blows kisses to me which I pretend to catch.

I watch them go with a heavy heart and wonder if I will ever get used to the situation that I am now in.

As I close the door the panic sets in as I realise that in less than an hour Daniel will be coming around for a night of X rated fun.

I rush around like a mini tornado and tidy everything away and light a few scented candles to disguise the smell of wet dog and shepherds pie.

I fleetingly wonder what I should wear. I mean it's not as if it's a proper date or anything. It is just two friends hanging out probably having a good old gossip and a bitch about everyone we know. Gay best friends are good for that; I read the magazines I know what it involves.

I decide on some black leggings and t-shirt with an oversized sweatshirt and my slipper boots. Hardly what I would wear normally for a date but as this isn't a date it doesn't matter. Despite it though I do make sure that I do my make up and brush my hair, I mean I do have some standards.

Almost on the dot of 8pm the doorbell rings and I try to ignore the fact that my stomach flips. Get a grip Sophie you don't feel this nervous when Simone comes around for a stitch and bitch.

I open the door and see the heavenly sight that is Daniel who is lounging against the doorframe looking good enough to eat, in a purely platonic sense of the word of course.

He smiles at me and I can't help but notice that he looks me up and down and a strange expression crosses his face. Immediately I feel anxious. Maybe I've got something on my face or an undiscovered wardrobe malfunction. Then he looks at me and smiles the most devastatingly gorgeous smile that I have ever seen.

"Ready to do battle Sophie Bailey?" I grin.

"Ready when you are Daniel Rainford."

I stand aside to let him in and he thrusts some beers and a bottle of wine at me. "Here you go fuel for the troops. Show me to my battle station."

I lead him over to the settee and whilst he sorts the game out I go and grab us some beers and quickly put some crisps and nuts into bowls for sustenance. When I get back he is all set up and I sit next to him gingerly feeling as if I am having an out of body experience as I picture the scene.

Daniel spends the next 30 minutes explaining how it all works and encourages me to have a go. It takes me a little while and I feel like a completely useless girl as I make a total mess of it.

Daniel isn't a teacher for nothing though and his patience is soon rewarded as I find my mojo. I finally relax into it and in between sips of beer I set about bringing his alter ego down.

We actually have a great deal of fun playing the game and I totally lose myself in it. I am actually surprised when the game ends and I realise that we have been "*at it*" for two hours solid.

Daniel leans back and grabs another beer. "You're a fast learner Sophie, I'll give you that." I lean back next to him and clink his beer with mine. "It's all thanks to my teacher. I never realised how much fun it would be."

Daniel smiles softly.

"You know you really should smile more Sophie it totally suits you."

I look at him in embarrassment and he laughs. "You don't like compliments much do you?"

I grin. "No I don't. I suppose I'm not really used to getting them so I don't know how to deal with them when I do get them."

Daniel looks at me in surprise. "That I don't believe. Surely your husband used to compliment you, before the split of course?"

I look at him and then laugh. "No Lysander wasn't very good at the emotional stuff. His idea of a compliment was saying the tea was nice, or you've done a good job on that paintwork." Daniel laughs. "Paintwork?" I grin. "Yes I always did the decorating. Lysander can't stand it and so if I wanted anything done I had to do it myself."

Daniel shakes his head. "Seems to me that you've had a lucky escape. You may not think so now but any man that doesn't compliment his wife and allows her to take on the DIY deserves to be shown the door in my opinion."

I take a sip of my beer and smile at him. This is nice a good old bitch about my ex husband with my new gay best friend. Just what the doctor ordered.

Suddenly I feel liberated and spend the next hour telling Daniel all of the things that used to annoy me about Lysander, from his morning bodily functions to that annoying habit he has of scratching himself in the balls every time he gets out the car. I also tell him about his lack of stamina in the bedroom and now the floodgates have opened I find that I can't shut up. This is actually amazingly good fun and I haven't enjoyed myself like this for ages.

After a while I decide to ask Daniel about his life instead. "So Daniel, now you know absolutely every last thing about me and my dysfunctional ex marriage what about you?" Suddenly he looks cagey and I remember how Sam told me that he didn't like people knowing about him. I say gently. "How long have you lived with Sam?" Daniel smiles. "About two years but we've always been friends I suppose it was the next step really and suits us both."

I smile. "He seems really nice and you must hate it when he goes away."

Daniel laughs. "Hate it, I love it. I get the flat to myself and don't have to clean up after him. I get to watch what I want on TV and don't have to accompany him out everywhere to strange bars and

restaurants. No when he goes away I get to do what I want for a change as he is quite full on as I am sure you found out even in the brief time you met him."
I laugh. "Yes he was a bit full on but nice. He is so good looking too; it wasn't hard spending time with him that's for sure."
Daniel doesn't say anything and just sits back and takes another swig of his beer.
"Anyway Sophie, are you ready to go at it again?"
I snort into my beer and already feel just a little bit inebriated as I uncharacteristically burp after the effects of the beer. In total shame I put my hand over my mouth and look at Daniel in horror. He laughs and nudges me so that I lose my balance. "I never had you down as a yob Sophie Bailey, there was me thinking you were a lady." I grin more to hide my embarrassment than anything else before saying,
"Yes well you are just about to find out how much of a lady I really am Mr prim and proper Rainford before I pulverise your virtual ass." He looks at me and grins wickedly. "Bring it on baby, I've got all night if you have."
I nudge him back and then we carry on where we left off.

Chapter Twenty Nine

The next morning I look around my house in total despair. The evidence of our marathon session is all around. Empty beer bottles and bowls litter the room. The cushions are everywhere where we had a cushion fight after the game finished. The various empty packets of junk food that we consumed lay around the floor that were then systematically demolished by Mr Tumnus.

Daniel left at about 2am. We had the best night that I can ever remember having and despite offering him the couch to sleep on he rang for a taxi to take him home. We were just a little bit drunk which can only explain what happened just before he left.

As we heard the taxi draw up outside Daniel took hold of my hand and pulled me towards him and kissed my cheek. His voice was soft as he whispered, "Thank you for the best evening I can remember having in a very long time. Just remember you are beautiful inside and out and never change." Then he stroked the side of my face and kissed me lightly on the lips before whispering, "Sleep tight Sophie Bailey and have sweet dreams." He then left me swaying in his wake as the most inappropriate thoughts flooded my mind.

I quickly check my watch and realise that I don't have long to walk Mr Tumnus before its time to head off to Annabelle's. I don't bother with hair and make up and just pull on my trusty tracksuit and head off. It is actually a lovely Autumnal morning and if Harry was here we would probably go and gather conkers or something.

I wonder what he will be doing today? Knowing Lysander he will be outright spoiling him and lavishing him with lots and lots of treats and chocolate to compensate for abandoning him during the week.

I don't blame him as I would do the same.

By the time I have walked the dog and tried to make myself look presentable it is time to go. Right then three hours of dust and grime coming up.

This time I'm taking no chances and grab my own cleaning bucket from the utility room. My nails need to survive the onslaught that is about to be inflicted on them.

As soon as I arrive Annabelle materialises and ushers me inside.

"Thank god you're here Sophie. We had some friends over last night and I'm afraid I haven't had time to clear up. You wouldn't be an Angel would you and start tackling it for me whilst I head off to my class?"

I look at the devastation in front of me. If I thought my house was bad this is a hundred times worse. Three hours just won't be long enough to whip this place into some sort of shape.

As she goes Annabelle shouts back at me. "Daisy is

at a friends and will be back at 1pm. I might be back but can you hang around if I'm not as I don't want her coming home to an almost empty house?" Before I can even think what almost empty means she shouts, "Oh Sebastian is doing his homework. He may surface but I doubt it, he's so dedicated to his studies."

Then she is gone leaving me in squalor.

I start the laborious task and after locating the bin bags set about clearing the rubbish that is piled on every available surface first.

Three bin bags later and I am beginning to see the scale of the gathering she had last night.

They must have got through a small off licence judging by the amount of cans and bottles strewn everywhere. Cartons of take away are everywhere some with the remnants of the food still inside. The smell is something else and I open the windows and doors to air the room.

I work hard and soon feel extremely hot and bothered. Despite this I am actually perversely enjoying myself and forget the time. I even manage to sing a little song as I work and worry that I am finally losing my sanity to find this enjoyable.

Two hours in and I am surprised to see Sebastian watching me from the doorway. Once again he looks at me with a hooded expression and just nods.

"Oh Hi Sebastian, do you want a cup of tea or something?" He grunts which I think means yes and instead of heading back outside he kicks a chair away from the table and sits down watching me as I make the drinks.

I decide to try and engage him in conversation. "So, good party last night?" He grunts again and looks around him with disdain. I try again.

"It must have finished late you must all be very tired." Once again he just looks at me and stares and I start to feel a little bit uncomfortable. Is this normal behaviour? Surely words work for everyone.

I decide to just talk to him anyway; maybe he isn't much of a conversationalist and just likes the company.

So for the next thirty minutes I whittle on about everything I can think of that might interest him. I even tell him about my Xbox escapades because surely he has one and we could bond over the latest war game. He just drinks his tea and dunks his digestive whilst looking at me as if I am a complete moron.

As soon as he finishes he pushes back the chair and leaves without actually having said one word to me at all.

I picture Harry and see my future. Is this what happens to our little boys? They grow up to be sullen teenagers and lose the art of conversation. I certainly hope not because otherwise I will most certainly have to get a flat mate. In fact come to think of it that may be necessary to help pay for things. The money that I am currently earning doesn't even come close to paying for the food we consume every week let alone everything else.

Suddenly I feel the panic setting in. What on earth am I going to do?

By the time Annabelle returns I have blasted my way through the kitchen and hoovered throughout the downstairs. The rubbish is out in the bins and I have picked some lovely dahlias from the garden and arranged them in a vase and put them on the kitchen table. Daisy returned home and I made her a cup of tea and found some wagon wheels to feed her. We had a lovely chat and I found out that she is hoping to start horse riding lessons tomorrow. Sebastian never showed his face again and as I hear the front door go I am elbow deep in washing up.

Annabelle breezes into the kitchen and air kisses Daisy. Who on God's earth AIR KISSES their six year old?

"Sophie my god you are amazing. Look at this place its fantastic, aren't you clever?"

I just nod. "How was your class?" Annabelle strangely looks down at her nails and then raises her eyes and mumbles, "Oh fine, anyway how about you? I heard that Lysander has taken Harry for the weekend again. It must be nice to have some *me* time."

I shake my head. "It's a bit strange really. I'm sure I'll get used to it after time."

She laughs shrilly. "My goodness what I wouldn't give for some *me* time at the weekends. Mine are an endless round of caring for this lot. You don't realise how lucky you are."

As I look at her it strikes me that actually it is her that doesn't realise just how lucky she is. A lovely home, family and her health. She may live in a dust palace but she is certainly Queen of it. She probably has no worries at all and if this is her idea of caring for her family then I wonder what it would be like if she stopped caring. Suddenly I very much want to get the hell out of here.

I start to gather my things and smile at her. "Well I had better leave you to it." She does that smile grimace thing and hands me the money. "Thanks again Sophie, same time next week?" Once again I almost see the desperation in her expression and just nod; after all I am going to need the money. "Of course. Have a lovely weekend. Bye Daisy, I hope that you get to ride the pony tomorrow." Daisy smiles at me sweetly and lisps, "Thank you for the tea Sophie. I hope that you get to have a ride too." Stifling a grin I wonder at what age the meaning of wanting a ride changes. If only that was going to be the case.

Chapter Thirty

I think about Annabelle and her family all the way home. Something doesn't feel right there and I'm not sure why. Why would she need to go to the country club at the weekend for a class and leave her children almost home alone? Surely the amount of money she is paying me could be saved if she only did it herself. Not that I'm complaining it's a godsend to me in my hour of need.

As I turn the corner to my cottage I am amazed to see Daniel waiting outside my front door. I can hear Mr Tumnus barking inside and as he sees me he smiles which almost makes my heart stop beating.

Suddenly I am aware of just what a complete and total mess I look after my scrubbing duties. He smiles in amusement as he takes in my appearance and the fact that I am carrying a rather large cleaning bucket.

"Well good afternoon Mrs Bailey. I can only wonder what on earth you have been up to."

I hold the bucket up and grin. "My Saturday job Mr Rainford. Us working women have to keep ahead of the game." He looks surprised. "I didn't know that you had a Saturday job." I laugh. "You didn't ask. Anyway it's only my second week cleaning for Lady Annabelle Range Rover Buckley."

I don't know why but he suddenly looks annoyed and then as I get nearer he appears to shake himself and just smiles. "Well Mrs Mop I was just picking up my car that I appear to have abandoned here last night and was wondering if you were up to a pub lunch. My treat as a thank you for such a delightful alcohol fuelled violent evening."

I laugh. "Yes I enjoyed it too. I am actually quite hungry but would feel bad if you paid. How about we go halves? I am a working woman now after all." Daniel just smiles and follows me into the house. Before I do anything I make a great fuss of Mr Tumnus and Daniel watches me with a sort of wistful expression. I look at him and smile gently. "You look like you would like a dog yourself Daniel." He smiles. "I grew up around dogs; we had several black Labradors mainly. I would like nothing more than to have another but it wouldn't be fair and anyway they don't allow them in flats."

Jumping up I lift up Mr Tumnus and hug him. "Well you can share mine if you like. How about we walk to the village pub and we can take him with us. Hopefully we can fuel even more speculation about our torrid affair and I can keep the gossip mongers happy for another week."

Daniel laughs. "Well I'm up for it if you are."

I hand him the dog and grin. "I'll quickly get changed and then we can go. I won't be long."

I race up the stairs two at a time and try to push away the thoughts of actually what it is that I would be very much up for.

Once we get to the pub we manage to find a seat in the corner and choose what to eat from the menus on the table.

The pub is your typical village one. Low beamed slung ceilings with various horse shoes and brass adorning them. There is a roaring fire nearby and a thin layer of smoke and dust clinging to every surface. The chairs and tables have seen better days, but despite all of this it is cosy and welcoming and I am glad to be sitting within its comforting walls with my dog and the fabulous man in front of me.

As we wait I tell him all about my Saturday job and the fact that I think it strange that I am there at all. He looks at me thoughtfully. "Have you ever seen her husband?" I shake my head. "No, I expect he is busy as he is some high rolling record producer by all accounts." Daniel looks at me and smiles. "No me neither. He never comes to the school plays or events and I only see Mrs Buckley at parent's evenings. Maybe she will bring him next week."

Suddenly I remember Parents evening and pull a face as Daniel looks at me with concern.

"I forgot about that. I will have to sit next to my errant husband and play happy families for the good of my son. I can't wait." Daniel looks at me sympathetically.

"Yes unfortunately he will always be in your life where it concerns Harry. That is why it is always best to get along, for the child's sake as much as anything."

Pushing away the unwelcome thought of a lifetime tip toeing around Lysander I just look around me and smile. "This is nice isn't it?"

Daniel laughs. "It sure is. Normally I would be down at the gym with Sam if he was home before heading home to get ready for a night on the town. This is much more my idea of how I would rather spend a Saturday."

I grin. "So Sam is into fitness then. I would never have guessed." Daniel looks at me and pulls a face. "So you have been checking him out have you naughty girl?"

I feel a bit flustered, because yes I had sort of noticed how gorgeous his body was but Daniel wouldn't like to know that I have been checking his boyfriend out so I just pull a face. "Not my type I'm afraid, I mean have you seen my ex husband? No I go for the middle aged, unfit, out of shape greying hair type that has never seen a gym in their life."

Daniel grins. "If he did then he may have had more stamina."

I almost blush as I remember all of the intimate details of our sex life that I spouted to him last night. "It was probably because he didn't really fancy me. I mean he has a younger model now so I expect he is working overtime."

Daniel reaches over and grabs my hand which feels really nice. "I told you before you are beautiful inside and out and any man that calls you his is extremely lucky in my opinion."

I smile at him in almost embarrassment. "You smooth talker Daniel, it's no wonder you're so sought after by the mafia."
He laughs and releases my hand just as the food arrives.

We enjoy a pleasant lunch and then reluctantly Daniel stands up. "Sorry Sophie I wish I didn't have to go but I have a prior engagement tonight that I can't get out of."
Jumping up I smile softly. "No problem, I must get back too. I need to get some shopping in and clean the house before the working week takes over again."
Daniel almost says something else and then thinks better of it and instead puts his arm around my shoulders. The feel of his touch makes me want to morph into him and never let go. Is it possible to fall in love with your work colleague so soon after your break up with your husband with a man who is in love with another man who you find equally attractive? Maybe I should call Jeremy Kyle to sort this out.
Daniel pays despite my protestations and as we walk back to his car he proceeds to tease me and try to push me over. I am grateful for the easy relationship that we have fallen into. Friends who enjoy each others company with no complications. This is what I need not some creepy guy in a bar with one hand up my skirt and one eye on the time.
Before he leaves Daniel smiles at me softly and once

again strokes my face. Leaning in he whispers, "Thank you Sophie, I've had a good time both last night and today. Maybe we can do it again soon." I just nod as he kisses me softly on the lips and then gets into his car and drives away.

Chapter Thirty One

I feel quite upbeat as I drop Mr Tumnus off and drive
to the nearby superstore. I have quite a lot of
shopping to get and so I may as well do it without
Harry demanding everything that he sees.

It doesn't take me long and soon my trolley is filled.
I actually can't believe how much food we get
through in a week. Not to mention the wine!

I also find food shopping quite exhausting. There
always seems to be someone there that I see in every
aisle and it becomes embarrassing as by the end of it
you don't know whether to say hi or not, or strike up
a conversation over the price of baked beans. There
are always hordes of screaming kids and it's always
my luck that I follow the naughty ones around.

In fact the noise levels in here today are off the scale
and with the various announcements and general
chatter I am getting quite a headache.

I decide that I really must embrace home shopping as
a matter of urgency.

By the time I come to pay I am frazzled. I now have
to load all of my shopping on to the conveyor belt
only to have to re-pack it at the other end. Then when
I get home unload it from the car and then unpack it
and put it all away. The process involved in shopping
is exhausting.

The cashier manages to get through my shopping and
I hand over my card and then punch in the number.

As I load the bags into my trolley she looks at me nervously. "I'm sorry madam but do you have another method of payment."

The line behind me goes quiet and it even appears that the screaming kids stop as it feels as though all eyes are on me. "What do you mean, why won't it go through?" The girl looks at me kindly. "It's probably a mistake; we've had a few today, maybe another card will work."

The trouble is I don't have another card on me and now I am starting to panic. Frantically I rifle through my bag and see with some relief the money that Annabelle gave me. A further rifle reveals my emergency £20 note and some loose change at the bottom of the bag. Thankfully I only have to get her to knock off the wine much to the annoyance of the queue before I am free to go.

As quickly as I can I leave the store with my cheeks burning and my head spinning and I know just who to thank for my humiliation. Lysander!!!

As I drive home the realisation sets in. He is going to make me pay for setting my solicitor on him and he is going to do it where it hurts. I will now have to watch every penny because one things for sure he wasn't joking when he said that he would make me pay. I didn't think it would be so literal though.

If I didn't have Annabelle's money then I would be seriously screwed.

I don't know why I feel so surprised. He said that he would bring it on I just suppose a part of me never really thought he meant it. How have we gone from being happily married to warring exes? My life no longer makes any sense.

As soon as I get home I put everything away and ponder my dilemma. I will need to speak to him about this and so I should try and at least be civil to him when he brings Harry back later.

Now my mind is set I start the cleaning. A tidy house is a tidy mind after all and I need mine to be immaculate when I face Lysander this evening.

As expected they arrive back at exactly 7pm. I wonder if he waits around the corner to time it so that he is exactly on time- I wouldn't put it past him. Harry races in and flings his little arms around me which surprises me as I usually come second to Mr Tumnus. "Mummy I'm home did you miss me?" I squeeze him tightly and just manage to say, "Of course more than I could bear," before he releases me and heads off to find Mr Tumnus who is conveniently outside in the garden.

Lysander looks at me warily as he pushes Harry's bag through the door. He nods. "Hello Sophie." With a deep sigh I fix him with what I hope is a welcoming smile and just say softly, "Please come in Lysander, I think we need to talk don't you?"

He looks surprised and looking just a little uncomfortable follows me into the living room.

We perch on opposite sides of the room and look awkwardly at each other. I try to look normal and start the ball rolling.

"We really should sort out this mess between us don't you think?" He nods and then smiles with some sort of relief.

"I'm so glad that you've come around to my way of thinking Sophie. I knew that you would see things my way in the end."

Trying not to let him irritate me I just shrug.

"Well obviously we need to make this as amicable as we can. What do you want to happen Lysander? I mean knowing you you have probably got it all worked out."

He smiles and starts to tell me how it's going to be.

"Well first of all I just want to say that I think you'll be quite pleased with what I have in mind. Firstly I will pay for the mortgage and all the household bills minus the food. You are now working so I believe so should be able to manage that. We will put the house on the market and when it is sold divide the profits equally. You can then start again and so can I. Harry can come to visit every weekend unless I have other plans which I will inform you of as they materialise. So there you go, no need to panic life will go on and we will just move forward as friends that share our wonderful son. So what do you think Sophie, happy?"

Well to be honest I wonder if murdering him on the spot would make things much worse because quite frankly I am gob smacked for want of a better word. I actually don't trust myself to speak without coming across as a complete psychopath. Luckily I am spared from answering as Harry bursts into the room and launches himself on me.

Lysander looks at us fondly and then jumps up seemingly quite happy.

"Well I had better get back we have plans this evening and I mustn't be late. I'm glad we had this chat Sophie, I will talk to the estate agents first thing tomorrow." He comes over and lifts Harry up and throws him high in the air much to his delight. "See you soon champ. Be good and the week will fly past."

Before I can even reply to his indecent proposal he is gone.

Chapter Thirty two

Simone is aghast when I tell her about my conversation. "The two timing, cheating, despicable excuse for a human being. How could he?"

I nod miserably. "He thinks he's being more than fair but there is no way on God's earth that I will be able to afford my own place. There is so little equity in the house all it would do would help me with the moving expenses. There's no way I can even afford to rent with the prices around here."

Simone squeezes my arm sympathetically. "I'm so sorry Sophie; you can't let him get away with this."

I slump back into my seat.

Simone is with me in the office after dropping Edward off. We haven't had a chance to catch up because she was away this weekend. I haven't even told her about my evening with Daniel yet.

Simone's expression softens. "Listen bring Harry and Mr Tumnus to ours this evening for your tea. We will work out a strategy. We won't let him get away with this. The most important thing is for yours and Harry's security going forward." I nod miserably and then Simone jumps up. "I'd better leave to you to it. I don't want to get you in any more trouble; you are going to need this job." I smile at her gratefully as she leaves me to my work.

As I start my admin I think about my situation. If Lysander gets his way we will have to move well away from here. Property to buy and rent in this area is through the roof. We may even have to move counties god forbid. The last thing I want is to have to move Harry away from his friends. It's bad enough as it is with his father moving out. This is a disaster.

I try to keep busy and when lunch time comes I am glad to get home and walk the dog. I very much need to be by myself at the moment to think about the mess that my life is now in.

By the time I return to school I am no further forward. To make matters worse it is parents evening tomorrow and I will have to sit side by side with my now hated husband in front of the forbidden object of my desires. Life is so unfair.

As I settle back down at my desk the door opens and Daniel comes in looking worried.

He closes the door and sits in front of me across the desk.

"Sorry Sophie but I just wanted to ask you something."

I look at him in surprise. "Of course what is it?"

He looks at me with a soft expression and says gently.

"Harry has told us that he no longer wishes to eat meat at lunchtime and he is now a vegetarian. Did you know about this?"

I look at him in shock. "No I didn't. He ate meat last week, maybe he's just messing you around."

Daniel smiles. "Yes you're probably right. I just wanted to run it by you because obviously it will have an effect on what we order from now on regarding the school catering."

I shake my head. "I'll have a word with him. I'm sure it's nothing. Sorry to cause you problems."

Daniel smiles. "It's never a problem where you're concerned. I kind of like dealing with your problems, they make mine look like nothing."

Despite how I'm feeling I grin. "I can't argue with that. I think I'd swap places with just about anyone at this moment in time."

Daniel looks concerned. "Do you want to talk about it?"

I roll my eyes. "No you've had more than your fair share of my troubles this weekend. Tonight it's Simone's turn to bear the brunt."

Daniel winks and almost gives me heart failure in the process. "Well just yell when you need me. I'm happy to be the bearer of the brunt as often as you like."

As he leaves I shake my head, why on earth is he gay?!!!

At the end of the day I meet Simone and we collect Mr Tumnus on the way to her house. She has kindly offered to make us fish fingers for tea which is actually one of my most favourite foods. It's funny how we love the bad things in life. I wish I could get as enthusiastic over pulses but no matter how much people tell me they're good for me I just can't warm to them. No anything coated in breadcrumbs does it for me every time.

The kids go off to play and we crack open an early doors bottle of wine to get the fish finger party started whilst I fill Simone in on every sorry cotton picking detail of my chat with Lysander.

When I finish she bangs her pans around angrily and I get a satisfying vision of Lysander's head under them as she pounds the surface.

"Well he can think that he's won all he likes. You tell Mimi everything he said and let's just see her agree to that on your behalf. You have a trump card honey. He doesn't know about your deal with the devil and thinks that you will jump at the chance to resolve this without paying out for a solicitor. Wait until he finds out that you are going all the way with this one and his happy ever after with his Ocean friend is going to be anything but when they are reduced to living in a camper van and eating out of tins."

I nod in agreement but still feel extremely unnerved by the whole situation.

Simone calls the boys in and we all sit down to a fish finger feast.

I notice that Harry is looking at his suspiciously and I remember what Daniel told me. "What is it Harry aren't you hungry?" He looks up at me and I see the worry in his eyes. "Mummy are fish fingers meat?" I laugh. "Of course not darling, why what makes you ask?" He looks serious. "Because Ocean said that we shouldn't eat animals it's not kind." I look at Simone who rolls her eyes and I try to brush it off. "Well fish fingers aren't meat so you don't have to worry. Anyway people have always eaten meat it's shall we say the law of the jungle."

Harry's eyes widen and Edward looks interested. "What like Jungle book?"

I smile. "Sort of. I bet that Mowgli ate the odd steak and burger you know." Harry shakes his head. "No daddy said burgers didn't count. He said that MacDonald's wasn't proper meat."

Simone grins at me. "He's got a point there."

I can feel the anger rising up within me as I picture Ocean messing with my son's head and if she was here right now I would tell her what I think of her. Instead I look at Harry and smile in a mother knows best fashion.

"Look Harry, some people choose not to eat meat and some do. You don't have to feel guilty though, sometimes we do things in life that under ordinary circumstances we wouldn't. However it's all a part of nature. Animals eat other animals to survive and have done since the beginning of mankind."

Harry still looks unconvinced. "Ocean says that we should only eat things that nature provides like things that grow in the fields and fall from the trees. I don't want to eat animals anymore. What would happen if we ate Mr Tumnus by mistake because we had run out of meat, I couldn't eat my puppy?"

Edward just says "Cool," and looks at Mr Tumnus in a slightly psychotic, killer of dogs way. Simone laughs.

"Well Ocean has her own reasons and we have ours. God made us the way he did Harry and you mustn't feel bad about that. You do what makes you happy little man. If you want to eat salad and vegetable risotto instead of sausages and burgers then good on you." She winks at me and I stifle a grin as Harry looks worried. "Don't they make vegetable burgers, Ocean said that you could eat anything these days and it doesn't have to be made from meat."

I am beginning to hate the sound of that husband stealing, son corrupting Trollope's name and almost can't trust myself to speak.

"Well yes you can Harry. I know why don't we try it for a week. If you like it we will give up meat. If you would rather carry on as normal we will do that too. For now though you can eat your tea without feeling guilty because the fish content in these fish fingers is virtually none, ok?"

With some relief Harry tucks in and then talks to Edward about some boy called Jason Mulligan who apparently has the latest Star Wars figure.

When they head off to play I help Simone with the washing up and sigh heavily. "As if things aren't bad enough. Now I'll have to devise a whole new menu around Harry just because Ocean thinks it's for the best." Simone shrugs. "Give it a few days and he will change his mind. He's only six and at an impressionable age. The lure of a burger and sausage will be too much to bear. You could always try frying some bacon that should cure him."

I smile. "Yes it always works for me. What if it doesn't though? Harry could grow up to be an animal activist and decide to live in trees. He will grow his hair and probably fall in love with somebody like Ocean who will take him away from me as well. Am I destined to lose all the men in my life to the children of nature?"

Simone snorts. "As if. Lysander will wake up out of the obviously drug induced haze that she has surrounded him with and Harry will move on to the next craze, my money's on Power Rangers. This is just a phase and you will have to suck it up and go with it because you cannot be seen to be the bad guy here. It will all work out in the end, just you see."

I nod in agreement and then lighten the atmosphere by telling her about my Xbox fun with Daniel and the subsequent lunch.

By the end of it her eyes are wide and she shrieks, "And you are only just telling me this. Oh my God he is so in love with you, I can't bear it"

I laugh. "Don't be ridiculous. I am his Judy Garland, Kylie Minogue and Lady Gaga all rolled into one. He is just being a good friend that's all."

I keep the kiss part to myself as I don't want to encourage her any more than is necessary.

Chapter Thirty Three

The next day I wake up with a firm resolve. I am not going to let Lysander bulldoze me into doing anything I don't want to. It's time to grow a backbone.

Before I do anything I dash off an email to Mimi telling her about the latest developments.

Now that is done I feel a lot better. I can leave my future in her safe hands and to hell with what Lysander thinks.

I feel happier as we walk to school. I even manage a quick rendition of Postman Pat for old times sake. It's good to know that I can get in before the playground mafia, at least that's one less thing to worry about. I know that I am still the subject of gossip, Simone tells me everything. Apparently Daniel and I are having an affair now and there isn't much teaching going on because of it. It would appear that we were caught-at it- in the staffroom by Miss Barley and had to explain ourselves to the head teacher. It was only because of her secret crush on Mr Rainford that we got away with it. Part of me admires their imagination, the other part of me worries that somehow they will be believed and Daniel and I could really lose our jobs.

It is only when we get into school that I realise with a sinking feeling that tonight is parent's evening. Lysander is coming at 7pm, as usual, and is meeting me here. I am dreading it as he is absolutely the last person that I want to spend any time with and especially in front of Daniel.

It is at morning break that Daniel pops in and I smile at him as he flops down in front of me. "Fancy a coffee Sophie Bailey?" I grin. "If you're offering Daniel Rainford, although I expect biscuits." He grins. "Coming right up."

It doesn't take him long and he is soon back with the welcome coffee.

He sits down opposite me and smiles. "So, what's the score with Harry is he a vegetarian?" I roll my eyes. "Apparently yes he is. Ocean has told him that it is unkind to eat animals and it is unnecessary. He now wants to eat only vege burgers and the like just in case we turn on the dog for sustenance."

Daniel looks concerned. "How do you feel about that?" I shrug. "It is what it is. I will go along with it for as long as it lasts. My betting is until Monday next week. That's about the usual time limit for one of Harry's fads."

Daniel smiles and I can't take my eyes off him. There is something deeply compelling about him, an intensity that I can't explain. If I didn't know that he was gay I wouldn't have believed it because the man in front of me has so much sex appeal he should hold a licence for it.

Breaking away I pull a face. "I'm dreading tonight. Just spending half an hour in my ex-husband's company is 30 minutes too many in my opinion."

Daniel looks at me reassuringly. "It won't be so bad. I'll keep him distracted with Harry's report and then he will be gone. I suppose it's a necessary evil."
The bell rings and he jumps up. "Anyway back into the fray fair lady."
I smile as he leaves the room but still can't shake off the knot forming in my stomach at what the evening ahead will bring.

Harry and I arrive at the school at 6.45pm and join the other parents waiting for their turn. Harry heads off to play with his friends and I am left on my own trying to look unconcerned as I look at all the seemingly happy couples around me. I can feel the stares and whispers pointed in my direction and try not to let it get to me. I haven't really spoken to anyone except Simone about my situation so I can't really blame them for making up stories. Everybody loves a good gossip and I am no exception.
Just before 7pm the door opens and my mouth hits the floor as I take in the sight of my errant spouse. I can feel the mirth around me as he struts into the room.
His once greying hair has been dyed jet black making him look slightly vampire-ish. He is wearing jeans and a t-shirt with a checked shirt that is undone. There is a leather type necklace around his throat that I instantly want to choke him with and one of those meaning type bracelets on his wrist. The worst thing of all though is the fact that he is wearing loafers

with no socks. I look up at him in disbelief as he nods towards me politely. "Hello Sophie, where's Harry?" I just wave my hand towards the school hall where the children are playing and he nods. "Oh fine." Instantly I feel annoyed. What did he think that I left him in Mr Tumnus's charge? I sit back and try to blank him out. I wish that he hadn't come. Seeing him at the moment is like pouring hot oil on sunburn. My wounds are still raw and open and every time I see him I am reminded of the situation that he has put me in.

He takes a seat opposite me and plays with his phone. Probably texting Ocean some love text or something. God I hate her.

Luckily we don't have to wait long before we are called in. Daniel smiles and gestures for us to take a seat. I feel happy to see that we have to perch in the gnome seats and I am looking forward to Lysander getting stuck in it.

Very politely Daniel tells us what I already know. That Harry is doing well and progressing nicely. He also mentions the fact that the school will be producing the usual nativity play nearer Christmas and that Harry has expressed a wish to be one of the sheep. I roll my eyes and grin but Lysander just shakes his head firmly. "Well you might not want to count on him being here."

Instantly my ears prick up and I look at him in surprise. "What do you mean?"

He smiles at me as if I am of a lesser intelligence.

"Well if the house sells we will have moved on. Ocean wants to move nearer her parents in the West Country and as it has a direct link to London we intend on moving down there as soon as we can."

I look at him in total shock. "But what about Harry?"

He smiles smugly. "Well I doubt that you will be able to afford to stay around here so as you have no other ties here you may as well move near to us so that Harry will have his daddy nearby. I know it's not quite Cornwall but it's near enough. It's all worked out quite well really don't you think?"

There is silence as we all stare at each other. I picture myself wiping that smug smile off his face with a baseball bat. I actually don't trust myself to speak and can feel the rage burning me up from within.

Thank God that Daniel is trained and he just stands up and holds out his hand to Lysander and shakes it. "Well thank you for coming Mr Bailey. It was good to see you again." He turns to me. "Mrs Bailey may I just have a word about the meeting tomorrow before you leave?"

I just nod and stay rigid in my seat, trying to digest what I have just heard. I can't even raise a smile at the fact that Lysander gets stuck in the chair and Daniel punches it a little too forcefully to the ground.

Lysander looks at me with a smug expression. "I'll wait for you outside with Harry. We have to agree a time for the estate agents to come around and take photos."

And then he is gone leaving me totally shell shocked

and completely on the edge of sanity.

As soon as the door closes Daniel drops down before me and takes my hand. "Breathe Sophie, take deep breaths and take your time." I can feel my eyes welling up and I look at his kind face and will myself not to lose it completely. "I don't want to move to the West Country. I might not have many ties here but I do have some. What will I have down there, he can't make me can he?"

Daniel pulls me close and I feel his heart beating against my cheek. He rubs my back and I melt into him savouring the comfort that he gives me. Pulling back he smiles softly. "He can't make you do anything you don't want to do. When you are divorced he will have no say in what you do with your life. Just make sure that you get custody of Harry and then you will be fine."

I look at him in alarm. "Oh my god he can't take him from me can he?"

Daniel smiles gently. "I don't think so but best to be sure. Contact your solicitor and tell her of your situation. She will sort it out for you. Don't worry everything will be ok in the long run."

He pulls me up and looks annoyed. "I'm sorry I've still got two more sets of parents to see. Why don't you take Harry home and I will pop by when I've finished here and we can talk about it some more? You've had quite a shock and it might help."

I look at him gratefully. "I'd like that Daniel. are you

sure you won't be put out though?" He shakes his head. "Never when it concerns my favourite girl. Go on put the kettle on and I won't be long."

As I walk outside once again I wish that things were different and that Daniel would be mine forever. I now officially hate my life but not as much as I hate my husband.

Chapter Thirty Four

I make out to Lysander that I have a headache and that we will have to discuss the arrangements another time. He wasn't happy but I don't care. I didn't even register the knowing glances from the waiting parents as I came out of the room. I no longer care what people think. Daniel is just a good friend and nothing else - mores' the pity.

I tell an anxious Harry that all went well at parent's evening and promised him a new toy for being good. The only thing that matters to me is him and I will put him before anything and always have done.

By the time Harry has had his bath and a story he is fast asleep and I am left to dwell on my increasingly bad situation.

True to his word Daniel knocks at the door at about 9pm. As I let him in he looks at me with concern. "Are you ok Sophie that must have come as quite a shock?" I nod. "You could say that. Anyway you must be exhausted. Let me make you a snack, do you fancy a beer or a coffee?" Daniel smiles gratefully. "You know you're an Angel. A beer would be great after the evening I've had."

I smile weakly and set about making him an omelette. As I work away he leans on the wall and watches me. It feels nice having him here and he doesn't take his eyes off of me for a second as he swigs his beer.

I feel the excitement grip me as I am aware of every breath that he takes but then firmly push down the forbidden feelings.

He looks at me thoughtfully. "You know you do have a say in what happens to you. Don't let yourself be bullied into anything." I sigh. "I have to keep on telling myself that. I suppose first I let my parents tell me what to do and then my husband. It just comes naturally to me. This is the first time I've had to stand up for myself and it isn't easy."

I plate up the omelettes and grab two glasses of wine and set them on the table. Daniel sits opposite me and scratches his head before smiling at me gratefully. "Thanks this is just what I need. A nice meal and the best company that I could wish for."

I laugh. "Don't let Sam hear you say that, he'll be jealous. I mean surely he's better company than me."

Daniel pulls a face. "No, I don't think he is actually. You win hands down on that front." I grin at him and we sit here eating in a companiable silence. It feels nice having him here and I don't even feel the need to make polite conversation.

When we finish he stands up and takes the plates to the sink. Turning around he comes over and pulls me up. "Come on I can hear that Xbox calling. You need to thrash it out on my virtual ass again."

I grin. "The way I'm feeling baby you're going down."

He grins. "Bring it on. I warn you though; I won't let

you win just because you're upset." I laugh.

"As if you would ever let me win. You're far too competitive."

I think its midnight when we call it a night. I look at Daniel gratefully. "Thanks for being here. You stopped me from dwelling on the sorry mess that is my life. You really are my knight in shining armour you know."

Daniel smiles and it almost makes my heart skip a beat.

"You make it easy for me Sophie. For some reason I feel relaxed around you."

He breaks off and scratches his head again and I raise my eyes. "Got a problem there Daniel?" He looks almost embarrassed.

"I hate to say this Sophie but I think I've got nits. They are rife again at school and this time I think I've got a dose."

I look at him and we both burst out laughing and then I joke. "The drawback to teaching infants." He pulls a face and I roll my eyes. "Ok as you've helped me out tonight let me return the favour. I've got some lotion and a comb in the bathroom. Do you want me to sort them out for you?"

He grins. "I will most definitely take you up on that offer but not tonight. It's getting late and you must be exhausted. How about I come over tomorrow after work and you can help me out then?" Suddenly he looks uncertain. "That is if you haven't got plans." I smile. "No, Harry has cubs and it is Simone's turn to take them. Come at about 5pm and the coast will be clear." He smiles. "Well if you're sure. It's a date then."

As I watch him go I very much wish that it was.

It must be at about 11.00am the next morning that Mimi calls me.

"Sophie its Mimi. What the hell is going on? I've had the most ridiculous letter from your husband's solicitor detailing some kind of settlement that you have supposedly agreed to. Didn't I make myself clear when we met? This guy is going down and I am beyond mad at these suggestions."

I grin into the phone as I hear the rage in her voice. She is so what I need right now. I stutter. "I'm sorry Mimi; he kind of caught me off guard. To be honest I'm not sure what I can agree to and what I can't."

There is a short silence and then she speaks, actually she yells down the phone. "I am going to tell that bastard solicitor where to shove his offer. There is to be no agreement between the two of you before you run everything by me first agreed?" I say meekly, "Yes Mimi." She sounds relieved. "Right then I will send them a return letter detailing our demands. In the meantime you are not to agree to anything and if he tries anything refer him to me. There is to be no house going on the market until the settlement is reached. You are to agree to nothing and sit tight and wait for the fireworks because he is going to be madder than hell when I have finished with him. Do you understand me Sophie?"

I say softly, "Yes Mimi, I'm sorry that I let him get to me." She sighs. "It's fine that's why I'm here after all. I am strong enough for the both of us. You just carry on as normal and tell me if he changes anything." I think about the money and say, "Well he has stopped paying me any money in my account for food. He says that I am working now and can afford to buy it myself."

The expletives coming down the phone even make me blush before she says wearily. "Well he will probably get away with that for now given your job. But don't worry I'll step this up a gear and try to move it on. You may have to reign in the spending for a little while as he is within his rights as he is paying for the house and bills. Just remember you're not on your own and there are procedures to follow in these cases. Just carry on as normal and keep me informed of every development."

I thank her and as I hang up I suddenly feel a lot better. Yes things are going to be a bit tight but I can cope with that all the time I get to stay around my friends. The thought of having to up sticks and move somewhere dictated to by him and his Trollope is just too much to bear. As I think about them I suddenly have an idea on how to make things just a little bit more uncomfortable for them this weekend.

Chapter Thirty Five

As I print off the letters about the nit epidemic I laugh as I picture Daniel with nits. They actually aren't that funny and take ages to get rid of. Come to think of it I had better check Harry just in case he has them too. In fact the more I think about it the more I can feel them crawling around in my hair. I start to itch and just wonder if it's me being paranoid. Maybe I should run the comb through my own hair later on just to be sure.

I am interrupted from my Nit drama by Simone who pokes her head around the door.

"Hi Soph um do you have a minute?"

I look at her in surprise. I hope she's not cancelling cubs; I don't want to have to put off Daniel.

I smile and wave my hand towards the seat opposite. "Of course what can I do for you?"

Simone looks at me nervously which instantly sets off the warning bells in my head. She never gets nervous so I look at her anxiously.

"Um sorry about this Soph but I have kind of got you into something and thought that I had better let you know."

I look at her and roll my eyes. "Go on what have you done?"

She grins. "Well you know that online dating site that I told you about?" Suddenly I see where this is going and steel myself for the bad news. "Um well I did sort of put your profile up and have had quite a few enquiries. I wouldn't be saying anything but some of them were actually really hot and interesting and to cut a long story short I have been kind of messaging one of them um on your behalf."

I sit looking at her feeling absolutely stunned and say weakly, "Oh no what have you done?"

She grins sheepishly. "Well I have sort of agreed for you to meet him tomorrow evening in town for a drink. He could only do Thursday because he is a fireman and has to work this weekend. I've seen his picture and he is like one of those guys off a calendar. I mean he is to die for and if his messages are anything to go by he has a personality to match."

I look at her in horror. "Oh my god you can't be serious, I can't meet him."

Simone looks annoyed. "Of course you can Sophie, he is exactly what you need to get over Lysander and distract you from this mess that you're in. I will have Harry and he can sleep over so if he is as hot as he looks and sounds then you must make the most of this opportunity. Oh my god if you don't go I am seriously thinking that I might. Opportunities don't come around this often and you so have to go."

I shake my head and she stares at me intently.

Shrugging my shoulders I say with resignation, "Ok what's the plan?"

Clapping her hands with joy she tells me what to expect.

"Well you're meeting at 7pm at the coffee place

opposite that wine bar we went to. You are to wear a pink scarf, don't worry I will provide that, and then he will meet you there and if you both want to take it further you could go for dinner at the Italian across the Street. Take your phone and if he's a total loser text me and I'll drive by like the cavalry and pick you up. Martin can look after the kids if I'm needed. There it's all been worked out. You can thank me later."

Obviously quitting whilst she is ahead she jumps up. "Anyway got to go, I need to prune my bush before the kids get home." She winks as she leaves and I just wonder who on earth does their gardening in the pouring rain.

The afternoon speeds past not giving me much thinking time and just before the bell Daniel pops his head around the door. "Still ok for later Sophie?" I smile. "Yes Harry is going home with Simone so come over whenever you like." He grins and then rushes back to class.

I wish he was coming over for more than a comb through. Life is certainly cruel.

Quickly I tidy up before Daniel arrives and try to make myself look a little bit more presentable than I am. Not that it matters as I am just a friend to Daniel but for some reason my body and heart just can't comes to term with that.

As soon as he rings the doorbell I open the door with

a flourish.

"Cornish Cottage nits service how may I help you?"
Daniel grins. "Who lives in a Cornish cottage in
Surrey? Only you would do that Sophie Bailey."
I laugh. "Silly isn't it. It stems from the fact that
Lysander and I used to go there quite a lot and fell in
love with the place. We always said that we would
retire there one day and keep chickens and donkeys.
You know embrace our inner eco warriors. The
trouble is Lysander has taken it literally and has done
more than embrace his latest eco warrior. Maybe he
forgot that I was part of the dream too."

Daniel looks at me with concern and I just roll my
eyes and laugh. "All of that is history now though.
The dream has become a nightmare and the perfect
life destroyed forever. Never mind at least we can rid
you of nits. That's one nightmare that I can control."

Daniel follows me inside and looks strangely nervous
and I look at him kindly.

"Listen don't worry it won't hurt you know. Why
don't I put the kettle on whilst you go upstairs and
wash your hair. There's a towel in there. I can do it
for you if you would rather."

Daniel grins. "Don't worry I think I can manage to
wash my own hair. I am a bit older than six years
old." I nudge him. "Maybe physically, but mentally
I'm not so sure."

I laugh as he goes off and for a moment it feels
strange seeing another man going up the staircase. At
least the image is of Daniel and he can go up my

staircase any day of the week.

My breath hitches when I see him coming downstairs towelling his hair as he goes. He has stripped to the waist and I gulp as I see his perfect body filling up my now increasingly small cottage. It is as though he moves in slow motion and it takes all of my concentration to tear my gaze away from his perfect six pack.

I swallow hard and try to focus on anything else that I can before he catches me panting with desire as I drink in the sight of him. Maybe a date is just what I need; I am obviously becoming some sort of sex mad beast in my singledom.

He looks at me and smiles sexily. "Well where do you want me?" He raises his eyes and I can feel myself blushing. In rather a high pitched voice I pull out a chair in the kitchen and squeak. "Here will be just fine."

I steel myself for what comes next as he sits in front of me. I start to comb his hair and hate myself for the perverted thoughts that are racing through my mind as I feel his hair run through my fingers. I try to picture Elton John in my mind to counteract the sexiness of what is happening in my kitchen.

Taking rather a bit too long to finish the job I reluctantly turn to the lotion. I splash it into his hair and once again comb it through before swallowing hard and saying, "There now we wait for a while for the deed to be done and then I will wash your hair and comb it through. Let me make you that drink."

I busy myself and every nerve end in me is tuned to him. I can feel him watching me as I mentally struggle to get a grip.

Finally I sit down in front of him and push the coffee towards him. "There nearly done. Hopefully it should do the trick."

He smiles thankfully. "Thanks Sophie, you're a godsend. Sam didn't forgive me for ages the last time I got nits. He got them too and vowed to move out if I ever brought them into the flat again."

I push down my disappointment at the mention of his boyfriend and just smile sweetly.

Suddenly he looks at me with a serious expression. "Are you ok Sophie, I mean it must be a lot to deal with on your own?"

I smile weakly. "Yes it is rather. I'm fine though. I mean hopefully it will all work itself out and we can move on."

Daniel looks worried. "Well we all know what that means to your husband but what about you, what is it that you want in all of this?"

I sigh heavily, looking at the most gorgeous man that I have ever seen in my life sitting opposite me asking me what I want and all I want to tell him is that it is him. He is all I want but it will never happen. Instead I just smile wryly.

"What I want Daniel is to be happy. I want to be in love with a man who steals my heart and rocks my world. I want to care for him and to be cared for by him. He must love my son as his own and put us before everything. I want to laugh and to live my life chasing rainbows and enjoy every minute of the time that I have. I want to be part of a team that sticks together no matter what. I don't want to have to worry that he will leave me for somebody else and I want us all to stay happy and healthy and be a proper family that loves one another and puts each other first above everything else. I want to find my soul mate and I want Harry to find his. I want the world for him and I never want him to feel any pain or be humiliated in the way that I have.

That is ultimately what I want Daniel but until then I will settle for just getting from one day to the next. I know that I am not ready for that all the time I am living with this uncertainty and pain. That is why I agreed to go on that stupid date that Simone set up for me with somebody that I have never heard of. Maybe for one night I can forget about my sorry life and escape from it all. I can be whoever I want to be and at this moment in time that is more appealing to me than anything else."

Just for a moment I see something flash across Daniel's face as I speak. He looks sort of lost and strangely vulnerable and I want to reach out and touch him. Then he appears to shake himself and looks at me with concern.

"What on earth are you talking about Sophie. What is this date you are going on?"

Laughing I tell him what Simone has done and he looks a little angry if I'm honest.

He shakes his head. "That sounds dangerous to me. This guy could be anyone. You can't possible go and meet him on your own it's not safe."

I shrug. "I'll be fine. We're meeting in a coffee shop and Simone will be on speed dial. If he's awful I'm going to call in the cavalry. At least it will beat watching Emmerdale."

Daniel still looks annoyed. "If I didn't have that stupid governors meeting tomorrow I would come and sit nearby to look out for you. Why don't you re-arrange it for another night when I'm free?"

I reach out and grasp his arm and he almost winces. "I'll be fine. Don't fuss. You forget that I can kick virtual ass baby. He won't know what hit him if he tries anything on. Either that or my rape alarm, always to hand when one is put in compromising positions."

Before he can tell me what an idiot I am I jump up. "Come on let's wash your hair and rid you of those little suckers."

I pull him up and he follows me to the bathroom. Once again I feel quite uncomfortable being with him in his half undressed state in the small compact space.

To hide my nerves I quip, "Right then bend over." He raises his eyes and I laugh. "I'll be your shampoo girl if you like. I always fancied being a hairdresser."

For some reason the light hearted atmosphere appears to have vanished and he seems withdrawn. I feel sorry that I laid everything out there; poor guy is probably so embarrassed.

By the time I have combed the dreaded nits out and he has got dressed it is time for Harry to come home. Daniel looks quite subdued as he heads towards the front door.

Just before he goes he turns around and fixes me with an intense look. I almost faint with desire on the spot as images of Poldark spring to mind.

"Be careful Sophie, I don't like thinking of you out there on your own."

I smile flippantly. "Don't worry about me Daniel, I'm a survivor. If I can survive what has happened to me lately I can just about survive anything."

Once again he throws me a worried look as he heads off home.

Chapter Thirty Six

I am on edge the whole of the next day. I actually
can't believe that I agreed to this and wonder if I
could feign an illness or something to get out of it.
The school is quite empty as they have swimming
this morning and by the time they get back I have left
for my lunch time walk with Mr Tumnus.
Simone has agreed to come with me to discuss the
plan of action for later.
As we walk through the woods she looks at me with
interest. "So how are you feeling about your date?"
I shrug. "Ok I suppose although I do feel a bit
nervous. I mean it is the last thing that I should be
doing. I was after all happily married just a few
weeks ago. How on earth has my life changed so
much in such a short space of time?"
Simone looks at me wryly. "I know it's mad isn't it?
It just goes to show that you never know what's
around the corner. You'll be fine though. Mimi will
sort out your divorce settlement and you can start
again. Who knows you may meet the man of your
dreams who also happens to a billionaire like
Christian Grey? Whoa fabulous sex for the rest of
your life in the lap of luxury, Lysander could have
done you the most massive favour here."
I laugh. "I doubt that very much Simone. Who is
going to want me? I mean I have nothing but a young
son and a puppy. I am penniless and fast approaching

middle age. No my future is to live my life through my son and look forward to the day I'm a grandmother."

Simone looks aghast. "Just you shut right up right now Sophie Bailey. You are in your prime and life is just getting interesting. You will ditch that baggage around your neck otherwise known as your husband and become the woman I know you can be. Onwards and upwards for you my dear and I won't hear another word about middle age and grandchildren."

We laugh and then as we reach my house I raise my eyes. "Ok I'll keep you posted on tonight. I'll drop Harry off after tea and then we'll take it from there."

Simone laughs. "How's the vege diet going?"

I grin. "Actually fine. I am enjoying it far more than Harry who is almost buckling under the pressure of vege pasta and salad. I give it two more days and if I dangle a sausage in front of him he may just take my hand off when he goes for it."

Simone grins. "Let's just hope that that's not the only sausage dangled in front of you; if Fireman stud's picture is anything to go by you could be partaking of one yourself tonight."

I push her and frown. "You are so crude Simone; I don't know why I am friends with you."

She laughs. "Because I say what you wish you had the balls to say. Go on get back to work and dream sinful thoughts to get you in the mood for tonight. I can't wait to hear all the juicy details."

By the time school has finished I have worked myself up into a complete bundle of nerves. I don't even see Daniel because he has been busy all afternoon and was then called in to see the Head just before the bell.

I try to keep my mind on my son and listen to him chatter excitedly about his day.

We have our vege risotto and then I station Harry in front of the television whilst I race to get ready.

After a frantic search through my mumsy wardrobe I decide on a smart white dress with black stilettos and a black wrap. I brush my hair and once again try to curl it like Zoella showed me how to on You Tube. A quick splash of Jo Malone and I'm ready.

Harry looks surprised when he sees me and smiles. "Mummy you look like a princess." My heart melts and I ruffle his hair. "You are my Prince Charming baby boy, always remember that." He screws up his face. "Yuk mummy, I'm not a prince I'm a soldier remember?"

I laugh. "Of course mummy's little soldier how could I forget." Pulling him towards me I savour the feeling of his little arms gripping me tightly. How could I love anyone more than I do my little man?

We are all soon on our way. Mr Tumnus is also going as it would be too long to leave him both in the day and in the evening. He will have great fun playing with the boys and I just hope that he can survive their onslaught.

Simone smiles at me when I drop them off. "You look amazing Sophie. I would go out with you myself."

I grin. "Let's not go there again Simone after our yoga session." She laughs. "Don't remind me. No tantric yoga is well and firmly in my past and that is where it will stay."

As I turn to go she shouts, "Remember I'm just a call away. I can be there in ten minutes if you need me. Stay out in the open and no snogging in dark alleys no matter how much you may want to."

I laugh as I head towards my car. She is incorrigible.

Chapter Thirty Seven

Ok now I'm feeling really nervous. I am draped in Simone's pink scarf and sitting in the coffee shop nursing a latte on tenterhooks every time the door opens.

I keep on expecting to see the fireman stud racing in in full uniform to put out my fire. Ok park the imagination this is real life after all. What if I hate him? I mean he can't be all that if he's looking for love online. All at once I feel stupid. I mean I am technically in the same boat even if I didn't volunteer myself for this dating nightmare.

Looking at my phone I see that it is 7.15pm and still no sign. Maybe I've been stood up. How much humiliation can one woman take?

Suddenly I hear a nervous, "Excuse me but are you Sophie?"

I look around and then do a double take. This can't be right. The man standing, or is he sitting I can't tell, beside me is nothing at all like I imagined. He looks to be about my age and is extremely small. He has brown hair that is combed neatly to one side and his green eyes look at me with a worried look in them. I can't even begin to describe what he's wearing; it appears to be a canary yellow knitted jumper with a BOW TIE! I feel quite ill as I look at him which he obviously notices because he looks down and mumbles, "I'm sorry Sophie, Zayn is running late and has asked me to come and keep you company. He has been called out to an emergency."

Zayn!!! Why didn't I think to ask his name? I sort of recover and smile at the funny little man softly. "Oh that's ok what's your name?" Bow tie man looks up and smiles with relief. "Oh my name is Barry." He thrusts a huge box of chocolates towards me and smiles hesitantly. "These are for you Sophie, by way of an apology for keeping you waiting."

Gosh how sweet - literally. I smile at him and wave towards the seat in front of me. "That is very kind of you or is it him? Anyway please take a seat; do you want me to get you a coffee?"

Barry shakes his head. "No that's ok, I'll go and order it, if you're sure you don't mind?"

I smile feeling bad. He seems like a really sweet guy and I hate myself for judging him by his appearance. He goes off and I look at the chocolates. They look expensive and once again I feel cross with myself. Poor Barry has had to go out of his way to keep me company for some love god friend of his that is off saving the world. I should give him a chance.

When Barry comes back he brings with him another coffee for me. He pushes it towards me and looks worried. "I hope this is what you like Sophie. I asked them to repeat your order, hopefully they got it right."

Even if they didn't I'm not going to let on. Barry is now officially the sweetest person that I have ever met and I am going to enjoy spending whatever

amount of time that we have together with him.
As he sits down I find myself staring down at him.
He must be only about 5ft tall and I wonder how
difficult that makes things for him.

I smile to put him at ease and he just stares at me in
total fascination. I am quite enjoying the effect I am
having on Barry, it's not often that someone looks at
me like they idolise me so I am going to lap this
attention up.

"So Barry, are you a fireman too?" He shakes his
head. "No such luck, I'm too small. I'm an office
clerk at the council. I deal with planning
applications."

I try to look interested. "That must be fascinating.
You must see some really cool applications for some
great structures."

Barry just smiles. "Not really it's quite boring. What
about you Sophie, are you a model or something?" I
actually now love Barry and am thinking of keeping
him to bolster my fractured ego.

"Oh Barry you sweet talker. No I am also a clerk of
sorts. I am the administrator at my son's school."
Barry looks surprised. "I can't believe you have a son
Sophie. Surely you are not old enough to have a
child? You must have been very young."

I wink at Barry and for a moment think that maybe
he is the soul mate that I have been looking for. He
says all the right things and has brought me
chocolates. Enough said!

Barry and I chat about general things for close on an

hour and then the conversation sort of dries up. I am starting to worry that my real date is not coming and start to fidget anxiously. Barry obviously sees this and looks at me a tad guiltily. Suddenly I understand everything and looking at him say gently, "Zayn isn't coming is he Barry?" He shakes his head looking embarrassed.

I grin. "He never was was he because you are Zayn aren't you Barry?" He looks at me with such a guilty look that I laugh out loud. Looking confused he says, "Aren't you angry Sophie?"

I grin. "Not really. I admire your cunning though. Now tell me what this is all really about?"

Barry looks shamefaced. "I can't find anyone to date me. Everyone at the office laughs at me and excludes me. They don't think of me that way and I can't say I blame them. I just thought that if I could get a nice woman to spend time with me she might like me despite how I look."

My eyes fill up and I reach over and grasp his hand. He looks at me in surprise. "Barry I like you very much. I have enjoyed our date and you are very sweet. Any girl that classes you as her boyfriend will be very lucky indeed. The trouble is it won't be me, even if you were Zayn it wouldn't be me, because the truth is I am already in love with another. The trouble is he can never be mine. So you see I do kind of understand your predicament because I too can only look from afar."

Barry looks at me sympathetically. "I'm sorry to hear

that Sophie." I shrug. "It's fine. I probably shouldn't be looking anyway because my husband has not long left me for a younger woman. Really I should just concentrate on sorting my life out instead."

Barry as it happens turns out to be an extremely good listener and I find myself spilling out every detail of the saga so far. Gosh this is like therapy. I feel tons better and find that I'm really enjoying myself.

Two coffees later Barry looks at his watch and looks wary.

"I'm sorry Sophie but I have to go now."

I look at him in surprise. "But its only 9pm are you due somewhere else?"

He looks a bit embarrassed. "I have to be home by 9.30pm otherwise my mum gets worried. She relies on me to help her to bed and I don't want her to worry as I'm all she's got left."

Once again my eyes mist over and my heart breaks for the kind, sweet little man in front of me.

To his surprise I jump up and hug him to my chest so that his face is firmly pressed against me. "Thank you Barry, I have had a lovely time. Give my love to your mother and remember what a great guy you are. Things will work out for you one day you know, I just know it."

Barry's eyes shine with happiness and he kisses my hand adoringly. "Same for you Sophie. I have enjoyed meeting you; maybe I can still email you from time to time."

I grin. "I would like that. Now off you go before your

mum gets worried."

As I watch him walk away I find that I am smiling.
What a lovely man.

Chapter Thirty Eight

As I walk to my car I think about Barry. Suddenly my situation doesn't seem as bad as he has obviously had a much tougher life than me. I have my gorgeous son and amazing puppy. I know I don't have much family but I have Simone and Martin and now Daniel and Sam. So what if Lysander didn't turn out to be the man I thought he was? I will be ok I just know it. Suddenly though my heart starts beating extremely fast and I can feel the panic starting to set in because walking towards me holding hands and laughing together is the very man with the woman who has stolen my perfect life. Lysander and the woman from the photograph- Ocean!

Frantically I look around me for an escape but it is too late because they see me and I watch as Lysander looks at me in total astonishment.

As they get nearer I try to look normal as if I always go for a gentle stroll every evening through the town. Lysander looks at me with a frozen expression and I see him gripping Ocean's hand tightly. I smile at him and try not to even look at the girl holding my husband's hand.

Lysander looks annoyed. "Sophie what on earth are you doing here, where's Harry?" He looks around him as if expecting to see him which really winds me up. Smiling sweetly I just say, "At a sleepover actually. Nice to see you Lysander." I totally ignore

Ocean who I can see looking at me in horror and disbelief.

Lysander growls. "What are you doing walking the streets on your own at night? Surely you should be caring for our son at home instead of palming him off on the neighbours." Thanking God for the laws against carrying guns in this country I just settle for the vision that I machine gun him to death instead before stepping over his body and kicking it into the gutter closely followed by hers. I actually can't trust myself to speak before an arm lands over my shoulder and I am pulled against somebody's side. I look up in surprise and am shocked to see none other than Sam standing next to me.

"Sophie darling, sorry I got held up. Come here you gorgeous thing." He then proceeds to pull me hard against him and absolutely kiss the life out of my mouth. He goes on for ages and I must say I am enjoying every minute of it. I can feel the shock and disapproval radiating off of Lysander even without looking at him which brings out the Devil in me and I run my fingers through Sam's hair and pull him even closer. God this is good, once again it's so unfair that he has a boyfriend. Fleetingly I imagine that I am kissing Daniel which really sets my soul on fire.

Finally we pull away and Sam grins at the staring couple in front of us.

"Sorry about that, this woman is like oxygen to me, I need her to survive. Sorry I'm Sam and you are?"

Smugly I wave my hand in their general direction. "Oh Sam meet Lysander and his new girlfriend." Lysander glares at me and Ocean just looks uncomfortable although the look she is sending Sam lifts my spirits even further. She is mesmerised by him and Lysander looks a very poor second best in comparison.

I smile at them. "Anyway we should be getting back darling." Sam grins wickedly. "Too right I've been looking forward to spending the night with you all day. Let's not waste a minute." He winks at the po faced couple in front of us. "Sorry guys you know how it is at the beginning. We just can't get enough of each other." He pulls me away and we try to stop from giggling like school kids until we are out of their sight.

I lean back against the door of a shop and laugh until I cry. Sam also laughs and says, "Did you see their faces. Round one to Sophie I think." I grin at him. "Well thanks Sam, I can't believe you came when you did. What a coincidence." He winks. "Not really, I've had my eyes on you all evening. Daniel told me about your date and sent me in his absence to watch over you. I must say though I was surprised at your choice of men." I smile. "Don't diss Barry he was an Angel. Don't be fooled by his looks his personality was solid gold."

Sam smiles. "It's good to see you Sophie. If I remember rightly I owe you an Xbox lesson." I grin. "Daniel beat you to it. I am now a master of said

device and can challenge the best of them."
Sam laughs. "Good on you. It's good to see you laughing though Daniel said things have been a bit fraught lately." He must see my face fall because he puts his arm around me. "Come on let's get a drink and you can tell me all about it."

Sam is also a good listener and I enjoy looking at his gorgeous face as I talk. He is also great company and I don't think I've laughed so much in ages.
Soon it is closing time and he walks me to my car. As we draw near he smiles softly at me. "You know what Soph I have really enjoyed your company tonight. Daniel told me how much fun you are and I have to agree with him. Just you make sure that you fight for what you want. Don't let your ex get you down because you are a strong woman."
I smile at him but feel my face fall as he reminds me of what a nightmare I'm living in. Suddenly though I feel a bit bad for Daniel. I have kissed his boyfriend and he may not like it one bit. I look at Sam anxiously. "Do you think that Daniel will mind that I kissed you, I mean I don't want to cause any trouble between you?" Sam grins wickedly. "Well what he doesn't know won't hurt him; let's just leave it as our little secret, I mean it was only one friend doing another a favour after all."
I smile with relief. "Of course, thank you Sam. It was good of you to do it. The look on Lysander's face was priceless and it did loads for my ego. You really

are an angel."

Sam winks. "More like the Devil Sophie."

I laugh and as I drive away I feel as if I have had a very successful night.

The next day I fill Simone in on what happened last night and she laughs so hard that I actually worry for her health. Wiping her eyes she splutters, "I wish I'd been there, just to see the look on Lysander's face when Sam kissed you. My betting is that he was majorly pissed about it and it completely ruined his night. What an idiot though trying to make you feel guilty about having a night out when that was exactly what he was doing. Maybe next time you should ask him to baby-sit. That would really wind him up."

I laugh but then look at her sadly. "I doubt there will be a next time. I mean I did enjoy it but I have realised that I'm not ready to date anyone yet. I'm not even sure that if Barry had been Zayn I would have felt right about it. It's probably best that I just concentrate on finding out who I am first before trying to replace Lysander. I mean I don't need a man in my life; I just need to find out what that life is now going to be. I should just get this over with and move on first."

Simone looks at me sympathetically. "You're probably right." Then she looks at me and raises her eyes. "Isn't it your birthday on Saturday though Sophie? 40 is quite a major one do you have any plans?"

I look at her sadly. "No, to tell you the truth I just want to forget about it. I expect I will have the dreaded phone call from my parents to look forward to and Harry will be at Lysander's so it will just be me and my dog and a mini bottle of wine."

Simone looks angry. "That isn't right. Leave it with me, I'll organise something."

I shake my head with determination. "Absolutely not Simone. I just want a quiet night in; last night was enough excitement for me anyway. I will just treat myself to Barry's box of chocolates and a DVD. I'll be fine don't you worry."

Luckily Simone leaves it there; to be honest my 40th birthday is the last thing on my mind.

Chapter Thirty Nine

Once again I don't see Daniel which I am actually
quite relieved about. He has had to attend a course
today and so Miss Barley fills in for him. I am sure
that if I was to see him the guilt would be written all
over my face at what I had done with Sam. I wouldn't
like it if my boyfriend had kissed another, even as
innocent as it was and I feel very bad about it.

When we get home I sit with Harry and watch a film
whilst we eat our tea on the settee for a treat.
I miss him at the weekends because that was when
we used to do the fun things like swimming and
cycling. I feel as if our life has fallen into a pattern
where I do the nitty gritty everyday things and
Lysander gets to enjoy the fun side of having a child
without the work.
Luckily we are having sausages tonight. Harry has
relented slightly and told me that sausages and
burgers are acceptable because Jordan Rivers told
him that they aren't made with proper meat. I'm not
going to argue with him there.
As we snuggle down to watch Power Rangers I
notice that Harry itches his head quite a lot. I really
should have run that lotion through his hair. It is
actually really good stuff and would get rid of them
almost instantly. The trouble is I am feeling quite
wicked at the moment and so instead I say sweetly,

"So Harry tell me, does Ocean ever read you stories?"

Harry shakes his head. "No daddy does, Ocean doesn't like doing fun stuff. She likes sitting on the floor and humming."

I smile to myself. "Well maybe she feels a bit left out. Why don't you make her feel better by giving her a huge cuddle and asking her to read you a story? I am sure she would love that."

Harry pulls a face. "Do I have to, she's weird?"

I stem the raucous laughter coupled with relief that threatens to burst out of me at his words. Instead I just smile serenely. "I'm sure she's really nice. Just ask her once and then you never know you might actually get to like her more."

Harry doesn't say anything else but I know that he will do as I said. He's a sweet boy and very kind at heart. He will soon be cosying up to Ocean and the thought fills me with happiness. Let's see how much she enjoys experiencing everything that goes with having a young child.

When Lysander comes to collect Harry the air is supercharged with an icy atmosphere. He almost can't look at me and I notice that he looks around him almost as if he expects to see Sam reclining on the settee naked. He obviously thinks I'm at it all the time and I am actually quite glad about that. Thankfully they don't hang around and once again I am left to my own devices.

I decide to have an early night, after all last night was a late one and I have my cleaning job to look forward to on my birthday. How the other half live.

I wake up on the morning of my 40th birthday next to my puppy. At least he is here so I am not completely on my own. The tears burn behind my eyes as I feel so completely and utterly alone.

Sighing I decide I had better get up and ready. The celebrations can be put on hold; after all I really don't have much to celebrate. I have no husband, a part time son and no money. My home is about to be sold from underneath me and I will probably end up in the West Country, far away from everything I know and pandering to my ex husband's wishes.

I have virtually no prospects and the only man that I can't stop thinking about is gay. My parents hate me and I am the subject of the local gossip for things that I haven't done. Well I suppose things can only improve - can't they?

I set about getting ready with a heavy heart and then the phone rings shattering my quiet contemplation otherwise known as depression.

With a sinking feeling I hear my mother's voice sounding strangely annoyed on the phone.

"Morning Sophie, happy birthday." I sigh inwardly. Only my Mother can make a celebratory wish sound like an accusation. "Thanks Mum, it's good to hear from you. How are you both?"

My Mum snaps. "Never mind about all that, when were you going to tell me that Lysander had left?"

My heart sinks.

"Probably when you called. I'm sorry I didn't tell you."

She sounds irritable. "Well thank goodness one of you thinks a lot more about us than the other. Lysander called and explained what happened and quite honestly Sophie I can't really blame him. You should work at a marriage you know, you can't just get complacent because then things like this happen. You have broken up a family now because of it and allowed a perfectly good man to slip through your fingers and all because you took your eye off the ball."

I am actually stunned right now and can't even begin to form a reply. Taking my silence as guilt she carries on relentlessly.

"I told Lysander that I was very sorry to hear it and that even though your relationship had broken down it didn't mean that ours had to. I mean he has always been like a son to us and the last thing we want is to lose him. Now I know it's your birthday and all but I want you to think about how you can win him back away from that young bit of skirt that is obviously satisfying him much more than you obviously were. Get a grip Sophie and fight for your man."

I actually can't take this anymore and for the first time in my life I hang up on my mother. How bloody dare she speak to me like that.

I ignore the phone ringing because I know it will be her. Instead I grab the lead and my padded coat and

head off for a long walk with my little furry friend.
So much for my parents, once again they have let me
down and I am done with them. Thank God they live
in another country because if she had been in front of
me spouting her diatribe then I would be arrested for
assault.

The trouble is why do her words hurt me so much?
It's always been the same. I have never been good
enough for her. All of my life she has found ways of
putting me down and making me feel lacking in
every way. I am sure that they just moved to Spain to
get away from me and there was never any love
shown towards me.

I used to envy my friends their Mother's who used to
do the things that I thought every mother should. I
envied them their close relationships and tried to
make excuses for mine.

The trouble is now that I'm a mother myself I realise
just how terrible my own one was and I suppose I try
extra hard with Harry to make up for my own
mother's shortcomings.

I never want him to feel like I do. I want to be his
world and for him to want to be around me. Once
again I feel so alone as I take my solitary walk
through life unsure as to what the future will bring.

Chapter Forty

As soon as I get to Annabelle's she is almost straight out the door. "Sorry Sophie must dash I have an earlier slot today. Daisy is at a friends and Sebastian needs your help with his homework if you don't mind. He wants to follow you around for some media studies project he's got to have in on Monday. Sorry to rush see you later."

I'm not sure I heard her right. Me help Sebastian with homework?

As I head into the kitchen I see Sebastian sitting at the kitchen table with a video recorder. He looks at me and nods and I smile hesitantly.

"Oh Hi Sebastian, your mum said something about a project you need help with." He just looks at me and nods towards the camera and then actually speaks to me for the first time ever.

"I need to film a modern day mum."

I am quite taken aback but something about the look in his eye makes me stop and think. He almost looks haunted and despite his sullen exterior I can sense that there is something not quite right. Maybe I will take this opportunity to find out a bit more about him.

"Ok then what do you need me to do?"

He just shrugs. "Dunno what ever you do normally."

I think about it and then smile.

"Right then let's make this the best modern day mum

video in the history of videos. I am going to make it my mission to get you an A*."

I don my apron and draw on my inner Nigella. Time to play for the camera. Sebastian takes his position and I set to work cleaning the kitchen. I explain everything I am doing in my best perfect housewife voice. I give out little tips here and there and try to inject a little bit of humour into it, not that I get anything back from Sebastian, once again he is silent. However I don't let that concern me. I totally get into my role and imagine that I am on Good Morning with Holly and Phil and even laugh at my own jokes as if they are really here.

After a while I decide to move it on a bit.

"Ok Sebastian how about we take the dogs for a walk and see what we can find to talk about outside."

Sebastian just nods or does he flick his hair, I never can tell.

We go via Cornish cottage and collect Mr Tumnus en route.

It doesn't take long before we reach the fields and let the dogs off their leads to run free. They have a great time enjoying play fighting and I look around for things to talk about.

I start talking about the various plants in the hedges, the sky and even the birds. I describe the season we are in and then turn my attention to caring for your dog. Gosh I am a master at this. Sebastian must have hours of stuff by now.

Suddenly my phone rings and I can see that it's

Lysander. Looking at Sebastian I smile apologetically. "Sorry Sebastian I should get this do you mind?" Once again I get no response but answer it anyway.

"Hi Lysander is everything ok?"

Lysander suddenly screams down the phone at me leaving me in total shock.

"Is everything ok you say, well you stupid bitch no it is most certainly not. You just had to mess everything up didn't you? We had it all worked out and then your bitch solicitor sent me a letter with your ridiculous demands. I am so angry Sophie I almost can't breathe. I have just had a call from the estate agents telling me that they have been unable to contact you to set up a time for photos. You're probably too busy screwing around to think straight if your behaviour the other night was anything to go by. Oh and do you know what the icing on the cake is? Well let me tell you. Harry has been so badly neglected by you that he now has NITS and he has so kindly given them to us. Now Ocean is beside herself because she can't kill anything and has had to go to Wanda's to get a herbal remedy. Not to mention the fact that her aura has been badly dented and it is your entire fault you total and utter stupid BITCH!!"

I stand here frozen to the spot just holding the phone in my hand. I can't even utter a reply and just look at Sebastian in shock. I can still hear Lysander ranting down the phone and for the second time today I just hang up whilst he is mid flow. Tears threaten to fall from my eyes as my head starts to buzz with everything I just heard. Then out of nowhere I am knocked completely off my feet by the two dogs that are still playing and I fall flat on my back. The phone falls out of my hand and when I recover I see the horror on Sebastian's face as he sees me sitting in the biggest smelliest cow pat ever known to man. My phone is sticking up from it like a flag and then to my complete horror and mortification I have a complete meltdown.

Suddenly I snap and an almost strangled cry comes from deep within me. I am now so angry that I have no control of what I do next.

Sitting on my throne of poo I just start laughing madly. Then picking up a handful of it I throw it as far as it can go as I shout.

"That's it I've had it- enough is enough. How dare he, how bloody well dare he. He calls me a bitch well who made me one that's all I can say. He did. It was him who decided that I was no longer of use to him. He traded me in for a woman half my age and he left me when I thought we were happy. I was living the perfect life cleaning and caring for him because we decided that would be best. Now he has gone through some mid life crisis and turned his back on twenty years of marriage for a teenage Trollope.

She meanwhile has not only stolen my husband but is trying to turn my son into a vegetarian. She is off nursing a damaged aura just because my son gave her nits that I conveniently on purpose forgot to tell them about.

Well hard bloody luck sweetheart welcome to the real world. You open Pandora's Box and have to deal with what's inside."

I pull myself up still ranting and pace around the field shouting. Even the dogs are sitting watching me fascinated by the show.

"And another thing, so what if I let my son go for a sleepover whilst I went out on a date. It wasn't the sexual fuelled one that he thought it was either. Oh no these days you date virtual perfect men who when you meet then turn out to be anything but.

Just because my date wasn't a total love god it doesn't mean that he wasn't the nicest man that I think I have ever met.

Oh no that wasn't good enough for me though was it? My life is such a mess that I have fallen in love with my gay best friend who does happen to be a total sex god.

So as you can see life is a bitch and then your cheating ex husband calls you one. So what if I don't want to sell up and move to the West Country so that his new love can be near her parents, what about my parents? Oh yes they as it turns out hate me too and blame me for not being able to hold on to my man. Oh yes everything is all my fault.

I am the one who now has to work around my son to get enough money to eat because my husband has two homes to run. I am the one who will have to buy all my sons Christmas presents from the pound shop this year because I have been cut off.

Yes I am a total bitch because I asked my solicitor to help me and tell my lying, cheating, despicable, two timing bastard of a husband to bugger off."

This feels so good and I am now empowered. This is so what I need, I actually can't stop now.

Oh and do you know what is the icing on the cake, the fairy at the top of the tree and the best thing for last? Well dear Sebastian it is this, today is my 40th birthday and I am totally alone.

My husband has taken my son away for the weekend, my mum ranted at me down the phone and there is not a card in sight. I only have one friend and I am now destined to live my life through my Kindle because apparently that is where all the action is these days.

I am the subject of fabricated gossip by the playground mafia who have nothing better to do than invent stories about my so called decadent life.

So happy birthday to me, here's to the next forty years where I will live in poverty and be known as the cat lady because I will have to resort to taking in strays for company because no doubt my husband will now be fighting me for custody of my son based on my shortcomings as a parent."

As I say the words a huge sob works it way out and suddenly the floodgates open. This is my life.

Covered in shit literally with one big almighty battle on my hands and nobody to help me.

I sink down on to my knees and ugly cry myself

stupid. I forget that Sebastian is here and really let it all out.

Mr Tumnus gets worried and paws at my knee and I gather him up and dry my tears on his damp fur. Suddenly I feel somebody sink down next to me and put their arm around my shoulder. I look up in surprise and see Sebastian looking at me with concern. He doesn't speak but looks at me with such a gut wrenching look that it takes my breath away. His eyes fill with tears and he says in a low voice, "My dad left too."

I look at him in shock and he shrugs. "He left months ago. Just walked out and never came back. We haven't seen him since but he phones every now and again."

I don't know what to say and just squeeze his hand. He stares in front of him and his eyes look dead.

"Mum doesn't want anyone to know. She has told us to say that he is busy working if anyone asks. She said that he is living with a man and if it came out then we would be laughing stocks."

I manage to say quietly, "It must be tough for you all." He nods. "Mum has had to work to pay for everything. He does send her some money but it's not enough."

Thinking about the state of their house and the cheap food it all begins to slot into place.

He carries on in his low voice.

"She doesn't know I know this but she has taken work as an escort to get money. That is why she goes off every Saturday; she meets one of her regulars who gives her lots of money. He's not the only one and I know that she works when we are at school. I think it's all she can do because my dad always paid for everything and she never had to work."

I can see the tears behind his eyes and my heart reaches out to him. My problems fade in an instant as I see the tormented teenager sitting next to me in a field surrounded by cow pats.

I smile at him reassuringly. "You know your mum is a brave woman. She is doing what she has to for you and Daisy. It can't be easy on her and whatever happened in her relationship with your father she doesn't deserve this, none of you do."

He looks down and I grab his hand. "Come on what a pair we are. Let's go home and I'll make us a nice hot chocolate. We can talk about it if you like. You can ask me anything and tell me anything you want. We have no secrets from each other now and everyone needs somebody that they can sound off to from time to time."

Sebastian smiles a rare smile and we set off home.

Chapter Forty One

We clean ourselves up and I make Sebastian a hot chocolate. We talk about both our situations for the next hour and it is only when I hear the car pull up on the gravel outside that I realise that I haven't done any work. I wink at Sebastian. "Listen let's just keep this all between ourselves. You keep my secret and I yours, deal?"

I hold out my hand to him but something about his expression sets the alarm bells ringing.

He is looking at his video camera in horror and then looks at me in total devastation.

"What is it Sebastian, did you wipe the footage or something?"

As we hear the key in the door he says fearfully, "I'm so sorry Sophie I didn't realise it and I live streamed your video."

I look at him in shock and whisper, "What do you mean, where did it go?" Sebastian quickly pulls me outside before his mother reaches the kitchen. "Its gone straight to You Tube, the school set it up for us to stream our work. I didn't know it was live and now everything you said is on the web."

I sink back against the wall feeling weak as Sebastian looks at me with alarm on his face.

I shake my head. "But nobody will see it; I mean you can take it down can't you? It's only a school thing and it's the weekend." Sebastian looks at the screen and visibly pales. "I'm sorry Sophie, it appears to be trending."

I look at him in total horror. "What do you mean trending, what does that even mean?" Sebastian points to the screen. It has so far had 10,000views and the figure is going up every second. It's what they call gone viral. I'm so sorry Sophie I didn't know."

He looks as devastated as I feel and then I remember what he told me. "What about you, did you record what you told me?" He shakes his head. "No, I turned it off when I sat down."

I let out a sigh of relief. "Thank god for that. Anyway I'm sure it's not that bad. Nobody of any significance will see it; I mean they won't even know who I am. It will be fine."

Sebastian looks doubtful. "I hope so for your sake Sophie. I think I've just made your bad situation a lot worse."

Annabelle comes around the corner at that point and says loudly, "Oh there you are, don't tell me you're still at it poor Sophie. Sebastian you've obviously kept her from doing her work, what am I going to do with you?"

I watch as he retreats within himself again and I feel so sorry for all of them. At least my problems are common knowledge, actually more common knowledge than I thought thanks to media studies. I know though that if Annabelle's secret came out she would never recover from it. Well I can keep a secret and if it does ever come out it won't be from me.

I feel bad when Annabelle hands me the money. She needs it just as much as I do. Fleetingly I worry about how she earned it. This is sex money and I am not sure if it's legal or not. Maybe I would be an accessory to prostitution. I'm sure that would go down well at my custody hearing.

After another reassuring look at Sebastian I quickly head home.

All the way home I think about Annabelle. For once my problems pale in comparison to hers. What must it take to sell yourself just to get by and keep up appearances? No matter how tough things get for me I am not sure that I could do that. I actually have a new found respect for Annabelle despite her mafia ways.

As soon as I get inside I decide to have a shower and clean off the evidence of my melt down. I can see the answer phone flashing and totally ignore it. In fact I pull out the plug to the phone as I don't think I can cope with another shouting match with Lysander and my mother.

No it's my birthday and I'll cry if I want to. I am going to have an evening in with wine and a good film to take my mind off of everything. I think I may watch Terminator 1 and 2 for inspiration.

I start to feel better as I let the hot steamy water from the shower wash my troubles away. I am going to be selfish for once and totally cut myself off from the world. Tomorrow will be soon enough to deal with the fall out from today.

I am half way through Terminator 1 when there is a loud knock on the door.

Groaning I jump up to answer it and Simone bursts into the room.

"Oh my god Sophie are you ok?"

I look at her in confusion.

"Of course why wouldn't I be?"

Simone looks worried. "I think you should sit down Sophie because by the looks of things you haven't got a clue."

Suddenly I feel worried. What if it's Harry, I knew I shouldn't have cut myself off. Fear grips my heart as I look at my friend and whisper, "It's not Harry is it? Oh please say he's ok."

Simone's face softens. "No he's fine; at least I hope he is. No your problem is a whole lot worse madam." She looks at my worried expression and pulls me down beside her.

"Sophie it would appear that you are an internet sensation and if I were you I would seriously check my Twitter and Facebook feed."

I shake my head. "What are you talking about? I can't anyway because my phone is covered in poo."

Simone jumps up. "Then take me to your computer. We don't have a minute to lose."

I quickly turn on the computer and suddenly images of my crying face fill the screen. It would appear that

Sebastian was right and I am trending everywhere. It is also on the BBC news website for god's sake.

I look at Simone in horror who looks at me in shock. You might want to stay inside for a bit. It's all over social media and you might not want to go on mums net for a while."

I stutter, "Why what are they saying?"

Simone pulls a face. "I think they've set up a forum for you alone, in fact there are now several. There are the ones that think you're a bad mother who neglects her son, there's the ones in support of you and against Lysander. Some are topical about mid life crisis and men with younger women. Oh in fact you name the topic and I think you pretty much covered it in your rant."

I slump back weakly. "My rant?"

Simone grins. "They are billing it as Sophie's rant. There's not a radio station or news channel not showing it. They've even sent a news van to the village who are currently interviewing everyone in the pub. I'm just surprised they haven't got here yet."

As she speaks we hear a loud knock on the door and I look at her in horror. "This is ridiculous. It's not news it's just a media studies project."

Simone raises her eyes. "Oh you know the gutter press. It is obviously a slow news day. What are you going to do?"

I put my head in my hands. I am shell shocked. I don't know what to do, why me and on my birthday as well?

In the end I do nothing. I don't answer the door and my neighbour Mrs Harrison calls the police who move them on. Simone makes me lots of cups of tea and I tell her what happened- minus Sebastian's confession of course.

We stay holed up in Cornish cottage for the rest of the night whilst we try to get our heads around it. Simone leaves in the early hours of the morning with the promise of coming back first thing. We decide to just ride this out. They will soon get bored and life will continue as normal.

Chapter Forty Two

I wake up in the morning and switch on my computer. It would appear that I am still trending and I groan. Steeling myself I plug my phone back in and see that there are fifty missed calls and twenty messages. Taking a deep breath I force myself to go through them.

There are several from my mother each one more and more irate than the last. Lysander's are equally angry and he yells down the phone for me to call him if I ever want to see Harry again.

I dial his number my fingers trembling and he answers it almost immediately.

"So you bothered to call at last. Some mother you are."

Biting back a vicious retort I try to keep my voice steady. "Is Harry ok?"

He snorts. "Like you care. I mean what mother goes online and posts a video to the world airing all her outrageous grievances online? Ocean is beside herself at being dragged into all of this and is inconsolable. You don't realise the damage you've caused."

I decide that I can't deal with him now so say shortly. "I'm sorry I've got to go there's someone at the door. I'll see you later when you bring Harry back."

He snorts. "If I bring Harry back you had better hope that I've cooled down by then."

I just hang up and punch a nearby cushion picturing it as Lysander's head. One thing is for sure he didn't see my side of anything at all in that video. I have definitely got a battle on my hands there.

There are some messages from various media channels all asking for a comment which I just delete. I can't listen to any more so just stop trying and put my head in my hands. This is a nightmare and I am now never going out again. If I thought that I was the subject of gossip before, this is off the scale.

Suddenly an icy feeling spreads through me as I remember what I said about Daniel. Oh my god he will be so angry. I've told the world about him and Sam in a roundabout way. Everyone that knows me will know that I was referring to him. This is now almost too much to bear and I bury my face in the cushion and cry like a baby.

Once again there is a loud knock on the door and I shout, "Go away whoever you are unless you're bringing me a stray cat. If you are leave it on the doorstep." I am now officially cat woman because that is all I can see in my future.

The knocking persists and I just cover my ears with my hands and choke on my tears. Lysander may get his wish yet as I will probably have to move as far away from this hellhole as is humanly possible. I will never be able to show my face again.

The knocking continues and then I hear Daniel's voice calling, "Sophie, its Daniel let me in."

I groan. Oh my god he's come to have a go as well. Will this nightmare ever end?

I crawl over to the door just in case there are paparazzi lenses trained through my windows and open the door a mere crack.

Daniel comes in and looks with surprise at me crouching behind the door. I quickly shut it and then stand up trying to maintain some sort of dignity as he looks at me incredulously.

I can feel my lip trembling as I look at him. He is so gorgeous even when angry and all I want is for him to hold me and tell me that everything will be alright. For a moment he just looks at me and I look at him. Words appear to be failing us both and then his eyes soften and he says softly, "Did you mean what you said Sophie?"

I look at him in confusion. "Which bit Daniel I said rather a lot as it happens?" He smiles softly. "The bit about being in love with your gay best friend." Immediately I colour up and look at him in total embarrassment. Nodding I say quietly, "I'm so sorry Daniel. The last thing you wanted anyone to know is now on every news bulletin out there. Are you and Sam really mad at me?"

Daniel just shakes his head in disbelief and the fear grips me. I don't want to lose his friendship.

He suddenly smiles which lights up his eyes and I stare at him totally mesmerised. "Sophie what on earth gave you the impression that I am gay?"

I look at him with a stunned expression.

"I'm sorry Daniel; Sam told me that you didn't want anyone to know about you two. It's why you keep him away from the school. I promise that I haven't told anyone."

Daniel looks at me incredulously. "Sam told you that I'm gay?" I nod.

"Well not in so many words but you must be." His mouth twitches. "Why is that Sophie?"

I look at him in total embarrassment. "Because you are well groomed and immaculate and caring and kind. You take time to listen to all my ramblings and are so on my level. You also talk about your life with Sam, of course you are gay."

Daniel smiles and looks at me softly. "I think you have got the wrong end of the stick Sophie. The reason why I listen to you and want to help you is not because I am kind."

He moves across and takes my hand. "It is because I am in love with you and have been for some time now. I have been doing the friend's role because you are not ready for another relationship yet as you confirmed to me when I came to get my hair done. I am trying to give you that time but it is getting harder because all I want is to tell you that I love you and want to be with you. I want to love and care for you and take your problems and make them go away. I want to be the person you want to be with and for us to be a team that puts each other first and have no fear of the other person leaving."

He pulls me close and whispers, "I want to chase

rainbows with you Sophie Bailey and all I need to know is if you want it too."

I can feel my eyes filling up again and my legs buckling and I can't believe this is happening.

As I look into his gentle brown eyes I feel as if it all makes sense. The man standing in front of me looking at me with so much love is everything that I want and more. He is my soul mate and I nod slowly and smile happily. "I do Daniel, of course I do."

Leaning down he touches my lips with his and as I feel the contact my feelings threaten to overwhelm me. He pulls me close and kisses me so gently and sweetly that it blows my mind. He pulls my head closer and then his kiss is deeper and more demanding and I don't hold back. Dreams can come true and mine is happening at my darkest hour. Finally it all makes sense.

After what seems like ages we pull apart and Daniel grins. "I've waited a long time to do that Sophie Bailey."

I grin back at him. "Well I've done just that in my head for months now, I am pleased to say that the reality far exceeded the dream."

Daniel laughs. "Well at least I'm glad that we cleared up the subject of my sexuality."

I blush and feel like a total idiot. Daniel grins.

"Sam told me what he overheard. He went along with it to teach me a lesson."

I look at him surprise and he laughs.

"I told Sam I liked you ages ago. In fact that first

time you came in after school when Lysander took Harry. I knew that it would be inappropriate to act on my feelings. You were vulnerable and having someone hit on you would be the furthest thing from your mind. So instead I made it my mission to just be there for you as a friend instead. Sam came to the school that day with the sole purpose of checking you out because I couldn't stop talking about you. When he heard your conversation he thought it was funny and wanted to teach me a lesson not to hold back because if I did I may lose you to another. When you told me about your internet date I was beside myself because not only was it potentially dangerous but I didn't want you to go out with anyone but me. I had that stupid governors meeting so I asked Sam to watch out for you."

I shake my head. "This is all so....well unexpected really." Then remembering the kiss I blush and almost can't look him in the eye.

His expression softens and he laughs. "Sam told me about your kiss and the act you put on for your ex and his new girlfriend. Even though I don't like the idea of anyone else kissing you except me, especially a rogue like Sam I did see the funny side. Your ex deserved the floor show and I was just glad that Sam was able to help you out."

Then he looks at me gently and pulls me close again. "Well Sophie what do you say? How about it, me and you against the world, a formidable team that can take on the mafia and the media. Put me out of my misery and say that you will be my girlfriend."

As I look at him I see everything that I want all rolled up into the gorgeous man in front of me who is looking at me as if I am the most desirable woman on earth. Reaching up I touch his lips with mine. "I thought you'd never ask. Of course I want to be your girlfriend Daniel. I know everyone thinks to the contrary but I'm not mad and you Daniel Rainford are everything I want in life and more."

We kiss again and I almost forget just how messed up my life is at this moment, because despite everything nothing else matters but Harry and Daniel now.

Chapter Forty Three

After lots more kissing Daniel pulls back and looks at me and smiles. "Anyway a little bird told me that it was your birthday yesterday so I have got a surprise for you."

Looking surprised I smile with excitement. "What even more than the surprise that you're not gay?"

Daniel grins. "Come on get ready, I'm taking you to lunch. No arguments you don't have a choice in the matter."

I look worried. "What if the press are out there? In case you had forgotten I am plastered across cyberspace at the moment having a complete and utter meltdown. I'm not sure that I can face anyone."

Daniel shakes his head. "Don't worry where we're going there won't be anyone looking at or gossiping about you. Come on we're already late."

Quickly I race upstairs to get changed. I wonder where we're going.

Daniel takes me the extremely short distance to Simone's house and I look at him in surprise. "Why are we here?"

He winks and knocks on the door. Simone appears almost at once and after pouncing on me for a giant bear hug she drags us inside.

"Where have you been? We've been waiting ages.

Daniel nudges me and I grin and Simone's eyes go as

round as dinner plates. "Oh my god you don't mean...?"

I nod and she shrieks looking between us. "I knew it, I told you he fancied you but you wouldn't believe me."

Suddenly she looks at Daniel anxiously. "You're not um gay are you? I mean if you are it won't matter some people like to swing both ways after all." I interrupt her, "No Simone Daniel is not gay I'm afraid I let my imagination run away with me and got it totally wrong."

Simone looks at us in relief. "Phew thank goodness for that. I mean it would have been a total waste after all."

I nudge her and Daniel laughs. Grinning Simone pulls me into her living room and I hear cries of, "Happy Birthday Sophie."

Party poppers go off and there is lots of cheering and singing. I look around me in disbelief as I see Simone, Martin and Edward standing next to a grinning Sam and of all people Barry. Tears once again spring forth and I look at them all in amazement. "Oh my god I can't believe it. And Barry how on earth did you get here?"

Barry smiles. "Simone e mailed me and invited me. She said that you were having a party so how could I refuse." I laugh as I look at everyone. "

This is amazing. I thought that this was going to be possibly the worst birthday I had ever had but it is turning out to be the best one ever. Thanks guys." I can't help myself and burst into tears. After the drama of yesterday it is all a bit much to take in. Daniel puts his arm around me and pulls me tightly against his side. "Come on Sophie, dry your eyes we haven't finished yet."

He pulls me down onto the nearby settee and Simone brings over a huge pile of presents. "Open these Sophie; I am dying to see your face."

Trying once again not to cry I start opening the beautifully wrapped gifts.

Sam has bought me the latest Xbox game and laughs at my excited expression. "Don't forget to invite me round to play with you guys. Being the third wheel isn't much fun you know."

I smile at him gratefully. "You're welcome anytime Sam."

Barry has given me a voucher for Costa Coffee and I smile at him gratefully. "Barry the chocolates were more than enough. In fact they were the only present that I got on my birthday and it was very thoughtful of you."

Barry blushes. "I wanted to give you something else Sophie, I hope that we will become good friends that can meet up for the odd coffee once in a while."

I smile at him happily. "Of course we can. I will most definitely hold you to it."

Simone jumps up and down with excitement. "Open mine next."

She thrusts a fairly small package at me that is beautifully wrapped and I open it carefully.

Once inside I laugh as I see a Kindle residing in a Cath Kidston case. She grins. "Loaded and ready to go with the Fifty Shades trilogy. May as well start you off on the hard stuff."

Everyone laughs as I blush deeper than Christian Grey's supposed red room. I can't even look at Daniel...what must he be thinking?

Edward thrusts a paper bag at me and says adorably. "Open mine Sophie I bought it with my pocket money."

I pull out a bar of chocolate that he has had personalised. It says, *Sophie is 40*.

Grabbing him I smother him in lots of kisses. "This is my most favourite Eddie; you are just too gorgeous for words."

Pulling back and wiping his face he yells, "Yuk" and we all laugh.

Daniel then hands me an envelope alongside a huge bouquet of flowers that he has pulled from behind his back like a magician. "Here you are Sophie, it's a bit of a selfish one but I hope you like it."

Mystified I open the envelope after admiring the beautiful flowers. I pull out a card and inside is a voucher for an overnight stay for two with dinner and breakfast in the nearby 5* country hotel.

He smiles as I look at him in shock. "Sorry Sophie, it's valid for a year so we can go when you're ready. I hope that you don't think I'm presuming anything, I mean you could take Simone if you'd rather."

I can feel everyone looking at me with amused

expressions and I just blush and then fling my arms around his neck. "Thank you Daniel this is amazing and the only person that I would think of going with is you."

I kiss him and just for a moment we forget that everyone is here until Martin coughs discreetly.

"Come on you two there's a massive lunch to get through and I'm starving."

We all head into the dining room and I am amazed to see that Simone has really splashed out and the table is groaning under the weight of more food than I have seen in my life on one table. The room is decorated with balloons and streamers and in the middle of it all is a huge birthday cake with a picture of me on it taken from the internet. It shows me having my complete meltdown and crying madly. There is a caption iced in a bubble above my head that says. *WTF now the whole world knows I'm 40.* I burst out laughing and everyone joins in as Eddie says, "What do the letters stand for mummy?"

One Year Later

Looking around me I can't quite believe that it's my birthday again. How the time has flown and so much has happened.

I laugh as I see Harry and Edward playing on the trampoline with Mr Tumnus. Luckily I invested in an enclosure so they are now perfectly safe.

My divorce came through and I am now officially no longer Sophie Bailey. Well for a few months anyway as I will soon be Sophie Rainford.

As I look over at Daniel trying to light the barbeque with Sam's help I can't believe that this gorgeous man is soon to be my husband. This time last year I had a lot to sort out.

Lysander never forgave me for outing him on the World Wide Web and it all got very messy indeed. Mimi turned out to be worth her weight in gold because she was strong enough for the both of us. I ended up keeping all of the equity in the house and Lysander has to pay me a large sum each month for Harry.

He even tried to sue for custody of Harry based on my supposed mental breakdown online. The trouble was Ocean left him soon after Nitgate and he ended up in a flat in town.

Apparently he is a frequent visitor to the Blue Banana after work.

He still sees Harry most weekends which I am happy

about as after all he is still his father.

Remembering the subsequent court case I have to laugh. The Gods were certainly on my side because it turned out that the Judge was none other than Annabelle's friend Frances from the Country club. She well and truly came down on my side and Lysander ended up much worse off as a result. Thinking about Annabelle I remember that she was totally amazed by what had happened to me and once I paired her up with Mimi there was no stopping them.

Her husband had a lot more to lose than Lysander and with those two against him he lost everything. Far from trying to keep a low profile Annabelle stood up to the playground mafia and managed to shift the focus of gossip from me on to her. She revelled in her new found notoriety, however they never found out how notorious she really was.

Her escort days as I believe are now well and truly over.

Sebastian got his A* for the media project and has now become invaluable to me as my assistant.

As it turned out I was an instant hit and following on from my melt down I was in great demand. I did the media tour of radio shows, magazines and even had a spot on Loose Women for a week or two.

Now *Sophie's blog* is one of the top blogs on mums net and my subscribers are fast reaching the 1million mark.

With my new found success came riches and what

with advertising revenue and my new book and DVD we are not short of money. Who knew that blogging was a career option?

Daniel applied for a job as a deputy head at a neighbouring Primary School which he is due to start after Christmas. We sold Cornish cottage and have bought a rather nice 5 bedroom house in the next village nearer his new school. I work around Harry and life couldn't be any better.

I smile as Simone comes over and hands me a fruit punch.

"Penny for them Sophie, you look miles away." I smile happily. "I was just thinking about how different my life was this time last year."

She laughs. "Yes it was rather. You've certainly come a long way." I nod. "Yes its funny how life works out."

Simone nods and then looks at me and pulls a face. "Did you get a card from your parents this year?"

I roll my eyes.

"Funnily enough yes I did. Ever since I've become famous in their eyes I can do no wrong. It's funny how they've changed their tune all of a sudden. They also love Daniel and have totally changed their opinion of Lysander. He is public enemy number one to them now, strange how they turned against him."

Simone snorts. "There's none stranger than your parents."

We are interrupted as the doorbell rings. Simone smiles. "That must be Barry; I'll go I can't wait to meet his new girlfriend."

She runs off to answer the door and I smile as I think of Barry. We meet up regularly for coffee and nobody was happier than me when he met Marcie his new love interest. They met at Wanda's tantric yoga class, still a hotbed for wanton thoughts and desires. I am glad that we got Barry onto it. Marcie is now his third girlfriend in as many months.

Daniel looks over and even from here I can feel the love radiating across the garden between us. We can't get enough of each other and life has certainly been like one of Simone's books for the last year. I grin as he comes over and he smiles sexily at me. "How are my girls then?" I smile and pat my rather large stomach in contentment. "A little tired and I think this one has hiccups." He laughs and holds his hand to my stomach. We have a little baby girl on the way in about two months time. We are delighted as is Harry who was only just a little bit disappointed that it was a girl. Now our family is complete. We have our latest family member to look forward to meeting and we have each other. As Daniel puts his arm around me and kisses me gently on the top of my head, I sink against him and look around me with contentment at my perfect life.

The End

Thank you for reading
My Perfect life at Cornish Cottage.
If you liked it I would love it if you could leave me a
review as it is the only way I can get my stories out
there as I have to do all my own advertising. This is
the best way to encourage new readers and I
appreciate every review I can get. Please also
recommend it to your friends as word of mouth is the
best form of advertising. It won't take longer than
two minutes of your time as you only need write one
sentence if you want to.

Have you checked out my website? There are free
books and giveaways on offer there as well as signed
paperback copies of all my books.

sjcrabb.com

Do you want Free Books?

Sharon Crabb is giving away a free starter library as
a thank you for buying this book.
(No strings attached.)

If you like FREE you can get your books here:

sjcrabb.com

Read on for a taste of:

The Diary Of Madison Brown
By
S J Crabb

Prologue

The music is extremely loud and there are more sweaty people jumping around than in a Gymathon! I can't find Ginge, typical! She is always going missing and I spend most of my time looking for her. It's not as though she ever worries about where I am, after all she knows that I am the sensible one and do enough worrying for the both of us.

I push my way through the heaving mass of sweaty bodies, trying not to touch anyone on the way. At last I think I can see her, she is dancing up on some sort of stage thing, ever the exhibitionist. "Ginge!" I shout, trying to catch her eye, "Ginge!"

"There's no need to be rude," says an irate voice in my left ear. I turn quickly to see a flame haired young man, about 18 I guess, glaring at me. He says angrily,

"If you want to get past you only have to say excuse me." Before I can even reply he storms off. Oh for goodness sake, some people are so sensitive; I didn't even know he was there.

Frantically I start waving to grab her attention. All around me people are dancing and singing and are, lets face it, drunk as skunks - although why they are referred to as such is beyond me, I mean I've never actually seen a drunk skunk have you?

Ginge, is my best friend and flatmate. She is not actually ginger, more a platinum blonde, with the disgusting figure and looks of a supermodel. Her nickname comes from the fact that she is called, Virginia Becton-Smythe, it got shortened to Ginge at school and has stuck ever since. Only her family call her Virginia.

We have been friends since school and live together in Parkmead - the new development of starter homes and flats in Esher. Ginge's parents bought her one for her 18th birthday - luckily they are loaded and couldn't wait to- off load her to her own space - it was probably cheaper than the cleaning bill as she is not the perfect housewife.

I live there rent free in return for doing the housekeeping.

Ginge is an Air Stewardess and spends most of her time on trips abroad, so it's like living on my own really.

No such glamour for me. I am a beleaguered sales rep for Scentastic, a company selling home scented products.

"Ginge!" I shout again and she suddenly sees me and waves. She cups her hands to her mouth and shouts, "I'm coming down!"

Shocked I watch as she leaps from the stage thing like a gazelle, gracefully flying through the air and landing beside me with a big grin on her face. Wow if I did that I would probably break a leg or something.

She shouts in my ear, "Come on Maddie, let's get a

drink!"

She pushes me through the sweaty throng using me like a battering ram until we get to the bar.

"Two J20's," she shouts to the bartender, who has miraculously become available, despite the crowd nearby vying for his attention. Ginge has that effect on men. They fall down before her like worshippers at the feet of Aphrodite.

"Are you having fun?" she shouts. I just nod; words are difficult in this environment.

We grab our drinks and find a seat nearby in a green leather clad booth. "God, I'm knackered!" she shouts at me, "I knew I should have gone to bed after the flight, but then it is New Years Eve after all, I can sleep tomorrow."

Just then - it's never long - two guys slide into the booth beside us. They look like Insurance salesmen, whatever it is that they are supposed to look like.

"Hey girls fancy a drink?" Insurance salesman no1 says to Ginge.

She flutters her eyelashes at him - oh here we go, I think with exasperation, she is such a tease. Ginge loves nothing more than toying with the opposite sex as part of some elaborate game that she concocts on our nights out. They don't stand a chance with her as she has a boyfriend, not just any old boyfriend either; he is only Rock God Tommy Carzola, from the Rock Band Crash & Burn. They met when the band flew first class on the airline that she works for. It was lust at first sight for them both and she arranges her work trips around wherever he is in the world on tour. She has just returned from Japan where they are currently touring.

"Thanks, we'll have another couple of J20's," she says smiling sweetly at him.

He almost runs off to get them and she turns her attention to his friend. "Hi," she says lowering her eyelashes, "my name is Amanda and this is Fiona." Nervously the lad coughs and manages to croak out, "Ian and my friend is Stewart."

"What do you do Ian?" she says slowly and huskily. He turns bright red and luckily for him Stewart arrives back with the drinks. He almost spills them in his haste to sit down and I smile at him trying to put him at ease.

Ginge picks up the drink and places the straw suggestively in her mouth, sucking the orange liquid up. Ian and Stew look at her almost panting like puppy dogs.

"So, what do you boys do for a living?" she asks them running her tongue suggestively around her lips.

"We work at Accisurance." Stew manages to stutter out whilst staring at her in total disbelief. I flash Ginge a triumphant look, I knew it! I can tell an Insurance person a mile off.

"What about you?" Stew stutters out looking disbelievingly at his friend.

"Well, we are set designers for Downton Abbey." Ginge says without missing a beat.

This scenario is typical on our nights out. We have been many names with many different jobs, from croupiers to film extras. I was an airline pilot once which was cool and Ginge's favourite is as a character at a theme park. She has been everything from Pocahontas to Minnie Mouse.

They look impressed and she is just about to launch into the full screenplay when the music stops and the DJ announces that it will soon be midnight and for everyone to take their places for the countdown. "Sorry Guys, must dash," says Ginge pulling me along with her like two modern days Cinderella's. We rush onto the dance floor and link arms counting down with the crowd.

3-2-1 - HAPPY NEW YEAR!!!

We hug each other and anyone else near us and all link arms for Auld Lang Syne. I notice the Insurance Salesmen trying to break through the crowd, but they don't stand a chance - luckily! I look around and then at my best friend. I love her to bits and feel so lucky that we have such a good life together. Maybe this is my year; I will find the man of my dreams, get the promotion at work and become the person that I want to be.

Now all I need is a plan.

January 1st - New Years Day

I woke up fairly early despite the late night. Ginge is still sleeping and probably will be until tomorrow. She has been known to sleep for 16 hours after a trip - especially one involving Tommy.

Ok, today is the first day of mission life plan. There is no time to waste. I must make this year count and need to know how to achieve my desires. First things first, Resolutions.

I grab my new notebook, the one that says Random Crap, and set about compiling my list.

1: Work hard and achieve promotion.
2: Save money and don't impulse buy.
3: Phone home at least every other day - not once a fortnight after a drunken night out.
4: Be organised at work and home.
5: Be kind to everyone - even Cardigan Darren!
6: Find everlasting love.

Ok, now I'm stuck. How exactly do people achieve their lifelong ambitions when they don't actually know what they are?

The phone vibrates and I can see it is Mum. I groan inwardly. Oh no am I ready for this so soon in the year? I answer the phone and whisper, "Hi Mum, I can't talk loudly, Ginge is still sleeping."

Mum just shouts, "Happy New Year Madison, will

we be seeing you this year, I mean we haven't seen you since last year?"

Mum goes off into peals of laughter; she says the same thing every year and still thinks it's hilarious. "Are you doing your New Years Day Roast Beef?" I ask hopefully. Mum and Dad don't live far so it wouldn't take me long to nip around for a hearty New Year's meal. "Yes, of course we are, it's traditional."

Happily I say, "Ok I'll be round about 2pm. Ginge probably won't make it though as we'll be lucky to see her at all today."

"Ok dear, see you soon - love you Bunny Boo." Oh my God I wish she would stop calling me "Bunny Boo." She thinks that it's her mission in life to embarrass me at every opportunity.

After I hang up I take stock of the situation.

Hmm, it's 10am 4 hours to go until lunch, maybe I should get dressed for the occasion. Looking down at my pink pyjamas with pandas on I think that I better had.

Right, New Year new me.

As I sift through my wardrobe I can't believe how many clothes I have that I never wear. Ok first rule of the year, wear something different every day until you have worn everything - or chuck it out.

That thought fills me with dread. I am a terrible hoarder and won't throw anything away. I still have my old school uniform from Primary School - of course it doesn't fit anymore but it has sentimental memories. Actually I hated school and school hated me, why do I want to remember it?

Spying some really cool leather look trousers that I had to have after watching Easy Rider, I decide on those with a leopard print top and fur trimmed jacket- fake of course, nothing is real in my life after all. Great, I look like a cool rock chick. Although I am not sure why I bought any of this really, it was probably after Ginge started seeing Tommy; we went to one of their concerts so I wanted to fit in. Jeans would have done it though- never mind they can be my new look.

I rummage through the shoe boxes under my bed and dusting off a large box I open it to reveal the leopard print boots that I bought and never wore, probably because they have heels. I'm a flats girl really.

Right, I had better not eat any breakfast otherwise I won't be hungry for lunch. I look at my watch and notice that there are still three hours before I have to leave.

Ok I'm bored already. I wish that Ginge would wake up. We could have a laugh and watch an old movie, Grease would be good, as I am embracing my inner Sandy.

Suddenly the doorbell rings sending me into a state of panic. Oh my God don't wake up Ginge!

I scurry to the door, fling it open and groan inwardly. Cardigan Darren, our next door neighbour is standing there trying to look cool and failing miserably. He has a very obvious crush on me, which I definitely do not reciprocate. He has sensible brown hair and glasses and always wears a cardigan - even in the summer - and is the most stylishly challenged person that I have ever met.

He looks at me nervously and plays with his fingers, which he always does when he wants something. His eyes widen as he takes in my outfit, hah he has noticed the new me, I think with a sense of achievement.

"Sorry Darren," I whisper, "I can't invite you in because Ginge is asleep. Happy New Year by the way."

He flashes a brief smile. "Happy New Year Maddie." Once again he licks his lips nervously. Inwardly I roll my eyes. Oh for goodness sake spit it out I haven't got all year.

Then I remember my New Years resolution to be kind to him, so I say gently. "How can I help you Darren, do you need to borrow anything?"

He blushes. "Only you, if you don't mind?"

Ok this is odd but hear him out before giving in to the urge to run inside and bolt the door. "Mind what?" I say encouragingly.

"Well, it's the Love thy neighbour service at Church today and we have been asked to invite our neighbours to come with us."

He must have seen the abject horror on my face because he carries on quickly. "Please say you will come? It won't take long and I'll buy you a coffee afterwards to say thank you."

Now normally I would do most things for a free Latte as I am kind of addicted, but Church!! He is looking so pleadingly at me that I can't refuse; it would be like kicking a puppy dog.

"Ok." I sigh resigned to my fate; maybe I might receive divine inspiration for my new life!

"When is it?"

"In half an hour actually so we should leave now, if you are ready," he says looking a bit worried at my would be Church outfit.

I smile inside, my inner Devil coming out, apt for where we are heading. I can't wait to see the Vicar's face when I rock up!

11am - Saint Bartholomew's Cof E Church

Well, finally we are here, walking up the gravel path towards enlightenment. Darren had wanted us to cycle here! I mean is he mad. Did he not see my footwear?

I had to put my leopard print foot firmly down, I mean the only way I could cycle here would be on Ginge's pink Pashley with a basket in the front, hardly Rock and Roll.

I told him very firmly that we would be arriving in my company car- well sort of, mine is in having some dents knocked out of it that some idiot gave me in the supermarket car park. He lost control of his trolley and it smashed into the side of my car.

Well I went off my trolley too, until I realised that he was actually quite gorgeous and gave me his number, for Insurance purposes only of course.

Well I am due to meet him for a drink to discuss the accident tomorrow evening. Oh well every cloud and all that.

I am driving the garage courtesy car. It is a VW beetle with, "*VW Forestford, for all your servicing needs*," emblazoned on the side. It has a really cool flower in a vase inside so I am thinking of asking to keep it.

Darren keeps on trying to hold on to me as we walk up the path, he is probably pretending that we are on a date. God forbid. Oh are you allowed to say that in the shadow of God's house? Actually you probably are, as I am sure his name is bandied around several times a day here.

The Church is really old and imposing, they should really make them more welcoming. I don't know maybe like a Costa or something with some little tables and chairs outside under church logo related umbrellas. They could serve up their messages on the side of small, medium or large coffee cups, I am sure that they would be inundated by customers then, and would probably make a profit. Ahead of us I can see the Vicar, resplendent in his white billowing gown. He looks a jolly sort, I might pitch my idea to him later, failing that he may need some scented candles for the vestry, they always smell musty. I bet women Vicars allocate a large part of their budget to scented candles and diffusers.

Note to self - pitch idea of selling to Churches at next Sales Meeting.

Seeing us approaching a broad smile breaks out over the Vicar's face and Darren grabs hold of my hand. I knew it the sly little cardigan wearing weasel, it was all a ploy to get me on a date, well 1/10 for the venue.
Not wishing to embarrass him in front of his idol I leave it in place, but stiffen my lips to indicate my disapproval.
"You must be Maddie," says the Vicar beaming at me, although looking a bit bewildered as he takes in my attire. God! -*sorry*- he even knows my name. Do they have confessionals here, what has Darren been saying about me?!
I smile at him warmly. "Good morning, I am pleased to meet you- my *Neighbour* Darren has told me nothing about you." Actually I didn't say that last bit, I just wanted to.
"Well I am pleased that you could make it at last, Darren has told us lots about you and how your busy life keeps you away a lot. Never mind though you've made it at last. We can have a nice jolly chat after the service."
What!!! I look at Darren incredulously. He blushes a

deep shade of red and won't look me in the eye. Snatching my hand away I go to speak but we are interrupted by a young woman heading purposefully towards us.

She is very slight and pale, with shoulder length brown hair held back by an Alice band. Oh my God - *sorry*- she is also wearing a cardigan. This is the cardigan club, if ever I saw one.

She doesn't look very happy and stands in front of us with a blank expression on her face.

"Hello Darren, who's your friend?" she says, with no trace of emotion or spark in her voice at all. Maybe she's a robot. She is looking at me, actually no, she is staring at me in the most unfriendly manner.

Darren shifts anxiously on his feet looking at me pleadingly and I suddenly totally get the situation. Miss Cardigan obviously has her sights set on Mr Cardigan here and for whatever reason he has, he has used me to put her off. Ok now I understand, it's time to put my game face on for my *friend*.

Grabbing Darren's hand I pull him beside me. "Oh Hi, my name is Maddie," I say in my best Ginge voice.

"I am Darren's very good friend and we practically live together." Well we do as only a wall separates our flats.

Oh God - *sorry*- I just realise that I am committing a sin in the presence of God, in his house actually. Well it's for a good cause namely Cardigan Darren. He shoots me a very grateful look which is the total opposite to the one that she shoots me as he quickly pulls me down the aisle towards a pew near the front and shoves me along quickly before the organ starts playing.

Looking around me I notice that there are actually quite a few people here. I am surprised that we are so near the front. There aren't many more seats, although Miss Cardigan manages to find one on the end of our row and is glowering at me as the organ plays, its dour melody perfectly reflecting my mood. God - *sorry*- it's cold in here, they really should get some heaters, maybe under pew heating, that would make more people want to come.

Mental Note: Pitch under pew heating idea to Vicar during Jolly chat.

The Vicar takes his place and starts droning on about friendship and the importance of neighbours. The only importance of neighbours in our house relates to the television programme. It's on Sky Plus and we have regular neighbourthons involving back to back episodes accompanied by huge Toblerones.
Why are Churches so boring? They could be so much fun if they just thought about it. They could have songs and videos, with films such as The Da Vinci Code and Raiders of the lost Ark. They could replace the pews with comfy settees with little coffee tables. Oh my God - *sorry*- the list is endless. I could

become a consultant for the Church Body and I would be single-handedly responsible for the Christianity craze that would sweep the land.

I smile happily to myself at the thought but then I'm aware of Darren nudging me, quickly I beam back to earth just in time to hear the Vicar calling my name. "Maddie, come on up and say a few words about Darren and what it means to be a good neighbour." Everyone starts clapping and I look at Darren in confusion, whoa what did I miss? Darren looks at me sheepishly and I realise that I have been well and truly set up. I glower at him but then part of me admires his nerve. He knows that I would have never come in a month of Sundays if he had told me. Well hats off to him, although I will have my revenge, and it will be sweet. I have to push past Miss Cardigan who smirks at me, probably hoping that I will make a complete fool of myself.

Ok! Time for full Oscar winning drama performance. I smile sweetly at her as I turn to face the Vicar who is smiling at me. As I pass him I dazzle him with my full beam and head up to the pulpit. I look around me pretending that I am picking up an award at a ceremony and smile happily at everyone. I can see Darren squirming in his seat, oh yes squirm away little Judas, you have every reason to be afraid. I touch the microphone to test that it is on in true Hollywood style. In fact I must be quite a sight in my Rock Rebel outfit with crazy hair. I haven't mentioned my hair yet. Well there's me and then there's my hair. It is a crazy blonde afro of the tightest corkscrew curls that hovers around my head defying even the most sophisticated straighteners on the market. I normally wear it tied up in some desperate act to control it, but today it is down and flying around me in all its glory.

Looking out in front of me I can see the sea of faces looking back, waiting to hear what I have to say. I have never been good at public speaking but am used to speaking to strangers - after all I sell for a living. Ok here goes!

"Hi everyone my name is Maddie and I am Darren's neighbour and friend. Stand up Darren and give everyone a wave." Darren looks at me mortified.

Revenge Step No 1: public humiliation.

He stands up quickly, waves and then hurriedly sits down. Oh no you don't treacherous neighbour.

"Come up here Darren, with me." I shout at him. He shakes his head, a look of horror on his face. Ha two can play at this game matey.

I wait, saying nothing until resigned to his fate he shuffles his way out of the pew and joins me in the pulpit. Everyone claps and I link arms with him - mainly to annoy Miss Cardigan who is glowering at me.

"Well, Darren is a great friend to have, nothing is too much trouble. I am always locking myself out so Darren comes to my rescue with the spare key that I have entrusted to him." Everyone claps. Ok now for step 2.

Revenge Step No 2: embarrassment

"Darren won't tell you this because he is too shy, but his hobby is massage. He gives a great full body rub - and he doesn't even charge. He does it for pleasure." Darren has now turned as red as a tomato and Miss Cardigan looks like she is about to expire. The rest of the congregation look shocked and the Vicar doesn't know where to look. On a plus point some of the women in the crowd are now looking at him in a new light. I'm really enjoying myself now, time to wrap up this revenge by escalating to step 3.

Revenge Step No 3: mortification.

"You see Ladies and Gentlemen, there are not many neighbours who would do your weekly shop for you for £20, to include the groceries are there?" Darren stiffens beside me anticipating what is to follow. "For those of you that know Darren know that he works at the local Superstore. I won't mention names as the Church doesn't advertise businesses."

Mental Note: Discuss advertising opportunities within coffee shop project.

"Darren selflessly gets my food shopping every week for me by bringing home £20 worth of past their sell by date food and beverage items. Without his generosity I would not eat as well as I do." The congregation look aghast but this bit is actually true. The food is fine and only just out of date, but it is always in its, Best before date, and we haven't had food poisoning yet so it must be ok. It saves us a fortune as well as the dreaded weekly shopping trip. Ok, time to redeem myself with God; after all I mustn't break my New Years Resolution No 5 on the first day. I turn to Darren and throw my arms around his neck, he looks afraid and awkward and I feel a sudden rush of love for him. He may be strange but he is still a great guy and totally deserves what will come next. "Thank you Darren, you are the best neighbour that I could ever wish for. There is probably not a person here who doesn't wish that you were their neighbour, I am the luckiest girl in the world. Then I plant a massive smacker on his bemused cheek.

The Vicar coughs, Darren now resembles a beetroot and Miss Cardigan looks like she has been sprayed by a skunk. Why is everything always about skunks? Do we even have them in this country? However the rest of the congregation give him a huge clap, some even offer a standing ovation. Maybe he will become the legend of, St Bartholomew's, and it is all thanks to me and my overactive imagination. We descend the pulpit victorious and once again push our way back into the pew.

The rest of the sermon is as boring as the first part; I call them the BM and PM periods, "Before Madison and Post Madison." Looking at my watch I notice that it is already 1.30pm. God -sorry, when will I learn? - Mum's Roast Beef!

2.30pm - Mum's Traditional New Years Day Roast Beef.

Well I managed to get out of the Church without further incident. I had to promise Reggie, The Vicar, a rain check on our Jolly chat and left Cardigan Darren amid a throng of interested women to make my way to Mum's for lunch.

She is in fine form even though Dad looks a little worse for wear. Apparently they spent the evening at, Elvis Chan's Chinese New Year Restaurant; Dad has to drink large amounts of alcohol to survive a night out with my mother. The lunch is sublime though. I always love my Mother's cooking and need at least an hours sleep afterwards before I can think about moving. I'm still a bit annoyed at her though as she doesn't think Rock Rebel is the sort of new image that I should be sporting. What does she know about fashion anyway? She thinks that Mary Berry's a fashion icon.

"So Bunny Boo, tell me your New Year's resolutions. Do they involve looking for a husband?

After all I was married by your age." "Mum! Please don't wish marriage on me at 25, most people now wait until they are at least 30 before they settle down. It's all about the experiences at my age." "You've been experiencing things for far to long in my opinion, how about experiencing married life and babies?"

I will never win this argument with Mum. I think she's just jealous that she didn't have as many experiences as I do so she's trying to curb my enjoyment.

Time to go I think. I have a sales meeting planned first thing in the morning and I have to drive for 2 hours to get there. It was obviously planned by someone who doesn't experience the joys of New Year!

6.00pm Packing for Sales Meeting

Ginge is still out cold so I am tip toeing around the flat trying to get organised for tomorrow. I have to leave at 6.30am to get to the Sales Meeting by 9.00am. I hope that the courtesy car is up to a long journey!

If I leave my clothes out ready I can get a bit more sleep. Now what shall I wear? It has to say successful business professional at the top of her game. There must be something like that in here. I pull out a navy suit. Hmm this may do - oh no I've remembered I wore that at the last trade show, it has to be something they've never seen before. What about that smart black shift dress with a green jacket? No, I think I wore that to the last sales meeting. The trouble is most of the time I wear quite casual clothes to work that say to my customers - non confrontational ,easy going, no pressure rep come to have a chat and you can buy something if you want sort of thing.

I know, what about that pink tunic with leggings and knee length boots? I can wear a smart jacket and my attitude glasses. That's it, I will look every inch the successful sales person- and they have never seen me wear it! Right, job done. Now I just need to look up the address on multi map - the courtesy car doesn't have sat nav - and I will be ready.

7.00pm Box set of Desperate Housewives/ selection box from Auntie Maureen

Ginge woke up so we decided on a marathon box set evening with snacks. Aunty Maureen always buys me a selection box - "You're never too old for these love," - she always says, a wise woman my Aunt. We love just sitting in our pyjamas tucking into chocolate and absorbing the lives of people that we aspire to be.

10.00pm - Disc 3

12.00pm - Bed!!!

January 2nd - Scentatstic Sales Meeting

6.30am! Oh no I should be leaving by now and I've just woken up! I'll just quickly grab everything and get dressed on the way. Luckily New Year's resolution no 3 helped me to be organised so I can just throw it all in and dress in the car.

7.30am!!! Gridlock on the M25. Everybody is back to work today it seems at the same time.

8.00am - driven 3 junctions. Haven't even been able to change out of pink panda pyjamas because an artic lorry is next to me and the driver keeps on looking at me and smiling.

8.10am - Lorry driver into sign language. I pretend I don't understand, why won't this traffic move??

8.20am - phone Matty my colleague from work. Have my headphones on so hands free.

"Hi, Maddie, are you here yet?"
"What do you mean here, are you there already?"
"Yes, they've even laid on bacon rolls - Betty has got the caterers in, it all looks really impressive. Where are you then?"
"M25, at least half an hour away."
"Never mind, Happy New Year by the way."
"Yes you too. How are the twins?" Matty and his

wife have twin boys, Lucas and Epheseus, I know, I blame celebrities for this weird name trend.

"Nightmare! Jemima's stupid bitch mother gave them each a drum for Christmas, another punishment present."

Matty's mother in law has never forgiven them for not calling the boys, George and Derek, after her father and husband. She keeps on finding little ways to punish them for defying her wishes. The boys are only 3 years old and shall we say a little bit challenging in the behaviour department.

"Yes it's been one hell of a Christmas. I got here at 7am just to get out of the house. I told Jemima that we had to stay over and have booked the Premier Inn for a night of alone time, just me and the TV, with a few Beers for company and possibly a pizza - heaven!"

I laugh out loud; Matty always cheers me up even in the most stressful of situations.

"Oh my God, there's a space with my name on it.

"Matty, stall the meeting for as long as you can, I'm finally on my way."

Isn't it unbelievable how traffic just melts away all of a sudden with no reason for the hold up? One of life's mysteries.

9.10am

Right I'm here! Just got to get changed and then I can head inside looking every inch the successful

salesperson that I am. Well I would have been if
Scent City hadn't gone bankrupt last year and cost us
thousands of pounds in unpaid bills. My figures fell
like a bungee jumper and I went from being top of
the pyramid to the bottom in one fell swoop.

9.20am

I CAN'T FIND MY LEGGINGS!!!
 I am sure that they were with the rest of the clothes.
Think think! Oh no, I remember now, Ginge was
cold and Mike had just got shot in Desperate
Housewives, she grabbed my leggings so that she
didn't have to pause it. Knowing her she is probably
still wearing them!
Ok, don't panic. Just keep your coat on and you'll be
fine.
 So I exit the car dressed in a pink tunic that barely
covers my best Primanis, with knee high boots and a
flasher mac. At least I have my Attitude glasses to
pull the look together. Luckily I have a scrunchie for
my hair. Good to go.
"Where have you been, you're late." Oh no it's Betty
Bulldog and she looks really cross. Betty is really
called, Elizabeth Bailey, and she is my Sales
Manager. We call her Betty Bulldog because she
looks like one and has a thin angry mouth that looks
like she has swallowed a wasp. She is quite scary
really and rules over us with a rod of iron. "Sorry
Elizabeth, didn't Matty tell you, the M25 was

gridlocked."

"No he didn't," she says crossly, "he was probably too busy polishing off the bacon rolls." At the mention of these I look around hopefully. I am starving and the breakfast bar that I ate in the car is a distant memory. "Well you're too late to eat anything now as we are just about to start," she snaps. "We have to get a move on because our guest speaker will be here at 11.00am along with the rest of the company."

I groan inwardly whilst maintaining a look of feigned interest. Betty loves her motivational speeches. At least if it's someone else we will be spared her attempts. Last time it was all about "Raising the Bar." By the end of it the only bar I wanted to raise was the one above her head before I knocked her out with it.

Note to self - Try to stop having murderous thoughts towards your Boss, not healthy!

"Anyway you can put your coat over there and then we had better start." Oh no, this is staying on me, for one it's freezing in here and I don't intend on flashing my best Primanis to my colleagues until I have at least had a few drinks. "Oh that's ok, I'll keep it on until I've warmed up a bit if that's alright?" Raising her eyes up she ushers me into the room.

There are about 12 of us Sales Reps and I actually

like all of them - unusual in this day of competition but we all get along great, united in our common hatred of Betty. I can see them grinning at me and I grin back like a naughty schoolgirl. Now I know why they look so pleased with themselves, the last empty seat is the one next to Betty. Oh well I don't blame them. I blow kisses around the room and head into the fray.

God, I'm so bored! Betty has been droning on about sales growth and opportunities for the last hour and it's really difficult to maintain an interested expression for this long, especially on nothing more than a breakfast bar.

Matty has fallen asleep. She can't see him because having been the first to arrive he bagged the seat on the end facing away from Betty. Oh well he probably needs to catch up with some sleep after living in toddler hell over Christmas. Oh no, she is moving to the flip chart, this looks like trouble.

"Now, I have posted up your sales positions on the pyramid. Well done Robert, you have achieved first place position. Maybe you could let the Team know your secret so that they too can reach the dizzy heights of No1 salesperson." We all clap and Robert looks around grinning. "What's my prize?" he says cheekily and Betty answers,

"It is being secure in the knowledge that you have a job for another year," she says looking hard at me as she says it. I can see my name on the chart residing firmly at the bottom of the pyramid. When I say pyramid, it is more like a block of flats really. I am firmly in the basement flat position which isn't fair. I am normally in the Penthouse position and it's only because Scent City went bust that I have plummeted so far down. Everyone knows it but Betty can't resist digging the knife in.

"Madison, we must have a talk about the opportunities in your area after your disastrous year, so please stay behind whilst the others head outside for coffee and biscuits whilst we wait for the rest to join us." She is now officially the Devil Incarnate. She knows that I haven't eaten and could murder a coffee. I look over at Matty in alarm and he reassures me via sign language that he will get me a coffee and biscuits. I so love Matty, he always knows what I'm thinking even before I think it sometimes. As they leave Betty points to my position on the board and circles it with a big red marker pen. "Doesn't look good, does it Madison?" I shake my head but think; I'm not having this it isn't my fault. Before I can even speak she rants on.

"You can't just blame Scent City for this, it is your job as a salesperson to anticipate potential problems and plan accordingly. Everyone loses accounts at some time or another but you have to have others waiting in the wings to take up the slack when they fail. I am disappointed that you didn't plan for this so I want you to go away and look for any potential that can replace this account. Now I must go as the guest speaker has probably arrived and you probably want

a drink - oh and lose the coat it's not Siberia in here."
I watch her click away in her four inch heels. She can
only be 5ft so she wears these huge heels to give her
an advantage. The trouble is she is so round that it
looks ridiculous. Heading outside I see Matty waiting
with the nectar of the God's that is a coffee with
some gorgeous looking biscuits. "Thought you could
do with this, oh and I pinched a plate full of biscuits,
here I put them in this carrier bag, they will keep us
going through the next hour or so of motivation."
"Thanks Matty, you know that you're my favourite
don't you?" I grin at him. Suddenly with horror I
realise that the whole company is turning up for the
speaker and Betty has left the flip chart in full view
of everyone with my name circled in red at the
bottom. "Hold this for me Matty; I have to do
something before everyone goes in." Quickly I race
back into the room. I'll just flip over the page and no
one will know. Why are these things so awkward? I
grab hold of the sheet and try to throw it over the top
of the board but it is so tall and keeps on falling back
down. Maybe if I jump up at the same time. No it's
not working and I haven't got long. Grabbing a
nearby chair I stand on it to get height advantage just
as Betty and her guest enter the room. "Madison!
What on earth are you doing?"
Startled I look around and the chair wobbles
precariously. Reaching out to steady myself I fall
against the Flipchart and it rocks dangerously. The
guest speaker races over and grasps hold of me and

then lifts me down in one Super Hero move. How embarrassing! I look up at my rescuer who can't be much older than me and is looking at me with an amused expression on his rather handsome face. Betty however is most definitely not amused. "Madison, what on earth are you playing at? Actually no don't tell me, I haven't got the time. Please for the last time take your coat off and then take a seat, and I suggest that you listen very carefully for the next hour because you of all people will benefit most from it." Hero Man looks at me, a smile threatening to break out but concealing it rather well in my opinion. Matty comes in at that point and seeing him Betty says, "Give Matty your coat, he knows where they go." Oh no I can't. "I'm still a bit cold; I think I'll keep it on if you don't mind." "Yes I do mind, I don't want you fidgeting around taking it off when the temperature goes up once everyone is in the room."

Ok you've asked for this. I slowly take it off and watch with great delight the horror that unfolds on Betty's face as she takes in my lack of leggings. The tunic literally just covers my bottom and with the knee high boots I look like a hooker. Matty snorts involuntarily and rather skilfully turns it into a cough. Hero man looks really surprised but Betty's face is like thunder. "Did you forget something?" she says now apoplectic.

Go to sjcrabb.com
for details on all of my books.
Subscribe and you will be
entered into a giveaway and can
download FREE books.

12011898R00168

Made in the USA
Middletown, DE
15 November 2018